SASQUATCH NIGHTMARE

BY

ERIC S BROWN

SASQUATCH NIGHTMARE

WWW.SEVEREDPRESS.COM

ISBN: 978-1-923165-42-7

SASQUATCH NIGHTMARE

Keith had made it. He was safe now. His back pressed against the cabin wall, breath coming in ragged gasps, he tried to force himself to calm down. The door was sealed not only by its lock but by a thick piece of wood laid through the bar that added to its strength. Shaking his head, Keith couldn't believe that Harry and Peter were dead. They were though. He'd watched them die.

It was Peter's idea to come up onto Harold Mountain and get away for the weekend. Keith wasn't a big hunter like Peter and Harry were but he'd figured what the hell? It was a chance to get so drunk he couldn't walk straight and have some fun. Keith worked too hard and would be the first to admit it. Unlike his friends, he was still single at the age of thirty-nine and didn't stand much of a chance at ever finding anyone to spend the rest of his days with. He was often jealous of them. They both had someone to come home to.

His right cheek was wet. Keith lifted a hand to wipe at it. His fingers came away covered in red. Keith stared at them wondering which of his friends the blood belonged to. Everything had happened so fast. Shaken to his core by what he had seen, Keith couldn't really remember the exact details of it all or at least they seemed twisted up and surreal inside his mind.

They arrived on Friday evening, hiked up to the cabin, got trashed, slept it off, and woke up to start drinking again. Peter and Harry dragged him along, out deeper into the woods. Both of them wanted to bag at least one deer for the day. And that was where things had started turning odd.

The woods were barren. There was no other word to describe it. No deer, no game of any kind to be found, at least by them, and, hell, what birds there were around seemed almost spooked. The worst of it though was that it didn't seem like they were alone.

Harry had been the first to work up the courage to comment on it finally, late in the afternoon.

"You feel that, man?" he asked Peter.

“Feel what?” Peter spat a gob of tobacco juice into the grass.

Keith had watched as Harry looked around before saying anything else.

“There's somebody watching us,” Harry said.

“Bull!” Peter laughed. “Ain't nobody else around for miles.”

Keith was inclined to agree with Peter. The truck they rode up in was the only one in the parking area at the start of the trail leading up the mountain when they left it behind. And they sure hadn't run into anyone else or seen any sign of someone else up here. They'd heard no gunshots from other hunters, saw no smoke rising into the sky from camp fires, or noticed anything else at all that would imply anything to the contrary.

“Yeah,” Keith added weakly, backing up Peter's take on things.

Harry glared at them. Keith had seen that he was really on edge.

“Look,” Harry said, “It's getting late and we haven't bagged so much as a damn squirrel. Let's just call it and head on back.”

Grudgingly Peter conceded. Maybe he realized just how freaked out Harry was, maybe he just didn't feel like a fight, or maybe Peter was simply ready to throw a few back. Keith didn't care. Seeing Harry so worried was enough to make him want to head back too. He didn't think there was someone out here like Harry but that didn't mean there wasn't some kind of animal stalking them.

Night was falling fast. The sky grew darker with each passing minute. A storm was rolling in from the west. Lightning flashed in the distance. Peter grumbled about the coming rain. Harry's eyes kept darting about, watching the trees around them. None of them really spoke as they trudged along towards the cabin. At that point, Keith's memory of it all got blurry. They heard something. . .something that had to be huge, tearing through the woods in their direction. Peter swung his rifle up to meet whatever it was. He never got off a shot. A huge, dark shape burst from the trees, knocking the weapon from his hands. Peter howled in pain from the damage done to his hands by the rifle being so violently and quickly torn from his grasp. His thumb was nearly ripped off and bent at an unnatural angle and most of his trigger finger was gone. Blood spurted from its stump. Peter was staggering backwards as claws gleamed in the light of the few stars that hadn't yet been obscured by the approaching storm. A huge, hair-covered hand grabbed him by the face, popping his head like a melon from the pressure of its grip. A shower of gore exploded over them all.

Keith heard Harry's rifle crack. He was shooting at the. . .thing. . .that had just killed Peter. Keith was ashamed of what he did. He ran like Hell for the cabin, leaving Harry to fight the beast alone. The thing roared in fury. Its voice utterly inhuman and unlike anything Keith had ever heard before. Harry's rifle cracked twice more in rapid succession. Keith didn't look back to see if Harry had killed the beast though, he just kept on running, his legs pumping beneath him. Sweat, born of sheer terror, slicked his skin and dampened his hair.

When he reached the cabin door, Keith finally looked back. Harry and the beast were too far behind him for him to see them any longer, but he heard Harry wailing before his cries suddenly fell silent. Something small and round came flying from the trees to hit the ground hard, bouncing, before rolling towards where Keith stood. He sucked in a terrified breath seeing that it was Harry's head. The sight of it got Keith moving again. He darted into the cabin and did his best to secure it.

Only a couple of minutes had passed but they felt like hours. Keith looked down at the rifle he clutched in a white-knuckled grip. He knew how to use it and the .30-.06 certainly was powerful enough to take down even most bears. Still, the gun didn't really bring him any comfort. Peter and Harry had been armed too and that hadn't helped either of them.

The night outside was silent. The only thing Keith could hear was his own panicked breathing. A drop of sweat dripped from his hair, splattering onto the cabin floor. His mind raced to come up with a plan to stay alive. He wasn't fool enough to think that the beast in the woods was gone. He was sure that the thing was still out there just waiting for a chance to get at him.

Keith couldn't move from where he was. His legs refused to respond to his brain. Fear had locked his muscles. He managed to slide a hand down to pluck his cell out of his pocket. Its screen lit up but Keith saw that he had no signal. The cabin was too far out in the middle of nowhere. It seemed like Harry had warned him about that.

He heard the thing coming, grunting, as it sprinted from the trees towards the cabin. It hit the door, an unstoppable juggernaut of primal power, and came crashing inside. Broken bits of shattered wood flew, several stabbing into the side of Keith's left arm and leg like shrapnel. The pain spurred Keith into motion. He threw himself away from the snarling, giant beast. The thing was so tall that its head scraped the cabin's ceiling, forcing it to bend ever so slightly.

There was nowhere to run to. Getting past the beast and out of the door of the cabin was impossible. Trying would only put him right within its reach. Keith was left with no choice but to stand and fight.

The barrel of his .30-.06 swung upwards as Keith braced the rifle against his shoulder. The beast was already stomping towards him. He squeezed the rifle's trigger. The high-powered round punched into the beast's wide chest, tearing into the thick muscle there. It did nothing to stop the creature though. Its hair-covered hands launched out to grab hold of Keith. The claws of one hand sunk into his shoulder, slamming Keith back into the wall behind him. The impact knocked the breath from his lungs. The beast's other hand came up from beneath him. Its fingers entered his flesh behind his scrotum while its thumb clamped over his manhood. With a ripping yank, the beast relieved Keith of his genitals. Blood splashed across the floor of the cabin and was slung onto the walls as the beast tossed Keith's package away. Keith was howling and screaming, thrashing about wildly in the beast's grip. The pain was so intense that his vision was blurred and only its sheer intensity kept him from passing out. Sucking in a ragged breath and fighting down the vomit rising in his throat, Keith got himself under control. Both of his hands grasped the hairy arm that held him, vainly continuing to try to free himself of it.

The last thing Keith saw was an all too human, if hideously animalistic, face leaning in closer before the sharp, yellow teeth crunched into the bone of his head. Then there was only darkness as the beast reared back, a chunk of his brain protruding from between its black lips.

****

Robbie woke up screaming, hair matted to the top of his head, slicked there by sweat born of fear. His right hand slapped to his groin, making sure everything was still there. Robbie toppled from the bed to land on his knees, promptly vomiting all over the carpet. Bits of undigested pineapple and pizza splattered onto his hands and lower arms. When his body finally stopped heaving, Robbie spat the last of the bile from his mouth.

Panting, Robbie leaned back against the side of his bed. The dream had been the most intense he'd ever had. Every moment of it felt so incredibly real. Using the bed to push himself up onto his feet, Robbie stumbled towards his bathroom. Flopping onto the sink, hands clasped on its sides, Robbie nearly tore it from the wall. It held his weight though and didn't break. Slowly raising his head, Robbie looked at his reflection. He was a mess. His skin was eerily pale. It took some effort but Robbie stood up straight and quickly washed the vomit from his hands. T he sunlight spilling in through the window made Robbie keenly aware of just how late it had to be. If his parents weren't out of town, one of them would have been banging on his door and yelling at him to get his butt in gear.

Robbie stepped into the shower and shuddered as the cold water he turned on washed over him. The water always took a moment to warm up. In a way, the cold helped him. It snapped him firmly awake and cleared away the ick of the night's horrid dream along with his sweat. Robbie was feeling a lot better by the time he was drying off.

Getting dressed as fast as he could, Robbie raced down the stairs with his backpack slung over his shoulder. He didn't stop in the kitchen to grab any kind of breakfast. Instead, Robbie paused only long enough to make sure the door was locked behind him.

He glanced at his dad's truck. Taking it might keep from being late but there was just no way in Hell Robbie was getting behind its wheel. He hated driving. Like most things, it scared the crap of him.

The bus had long come and gone. Robbie took off at a full out run in the direction of the school, thankful that he didn't live too far from it. His legs pumping, Robbie pushed his body for all the speed it could muster.

Standing on the steps of the school, Warren saw him coming and burst into laughter. Alison was with him. Her lips drooped as she frowned.

“You're an idiot,” Warren managed to get out between laughs.

“Rob,” Alison shook her head. “You missed first period again. Mr. Freer is. . .”

“Gonna flunk me,” Robbie said, “I know.”

“You're lucky he doesn't kick your butt good, buddy,” Warren snorted. “I mean, you stand the man up all the time.”

“Rob, seriously,” Alison scolded him, “You need to be thinking about your grades.”

Robbie knew both of them were right. It wasn't like he planned on almost always being late to first period and most of the time, he didn't miss it entirely like today.

“Come on, guys,” He pleaded. “I got here as soon as I could. My folks are out of town.”

“Ah, you didn't have a ride?” Warren puffed out his lower lip in an infantile gesture. “Poor baby.”

Alison sighed. “That's enough, Warren. What's done is done. And he is going to do better.”

“You bet I am,” Robbie lied through his teeth, flashing her an insincere smile.

The three of them headed back into the building. Checking his watch, Robbie saw that they still had a few minutes until the bell rung and second period started.

“See you at lunch?” Alison asked.

Robbie nodded.

He and Warren watched as she disappeared into the crowded corridor racing away towards her next class. The two of them had gym second period so they headed in a different direction.

“She let you off easy if you ask me,” Warren slapped him on the back.

“I didn't,” Robbie scowled at his supposed best friend.

“Mr. Freer isn't gonna,” Warren added.

Robbie didn't want to think about that. The

short, burly teacher intimidated him enough without being in the fit of rage he was sure to be in.

"So. . ." Warren stopped him and looked him in the eye. "This weekend?"

"I don't know, Warren," Robbie shrugged. "I'm still thinking about it."

"What's to think about, man?" Warren urged. "This is our chance, Robbie! We might not get another one, ya know? We've been outcasts for how long? Our entire academic careers? This weekend could change that, man. I know it."

"It's not your house we'd be putting at risk, Warren," Robbie answered. "I mean, my parents. . ."

"Are out of town," Warren cut him off. "If we have the party on Friday night like we talked about, we would have all of Saturday to clean up before your parents ever get home. And I am serious, man. This really could make us. If you say yes, I know I can score us some booze and weed."

"And that's supposed to make me feel better about it?" Robbie glared at his friend.

"It will when you try it, my friend," Warren put his hands on his shoulders, grinning like an idiot.

"Fine," Robbie batted Warren's hands away. "I'll agree to this party on one condition."

"Name it!" Warren yelped, nearly trembling with excitement.

"I'll do this if and only if you let me be the one who invites people," Robbie told him.

"Wait? I don't get to invite anyone?" Warren asked.

"Nope," Robbie shook his head. "You'll have to trust me to get it done."

"This is the only way you'll agree?" Warren eyed him closely.

"Yep," Robbie nodded.

"Alright," Warren said and then began to smile widely again, "Alright, alright, alright!"

****

Deputy Quinton was clicking away like mad with his cell, taking photo after photo of the body. Sheriff Amos just stood staring at it. It was the fourth this week.

The cow that lay in the field in front of them was badly mauled. Something had snapped its freaking neck. Somehow just breaking it with what appeared to be nothing more than brute strength. The white of bone stuck out through the flesh of its throat. Amos couldn't think of a single dang animal that could do that and surely it had to be impossible for any human to be that strong. The messed up mystery didn't stop there though. The cow was gutted, stomach ripped open. Something had eaten a good portion of its innards and the purple chords of its remaining intestines spilled out of the cow's open belly into the grass. The cow's legs were all gnawed on too. Large sections of meat chewed away from the bone. The heat hadn't been kind to the corpse either. The thing stunk to high heavens and there were already maggots swarming it. Days like these made Sheriff Amos question his life choices sometimes. His dad had always told him he should have been a trucker and maybe, just maybe the old man had been right. At least he wouldn't have the safety of the town and everyone in it weighing on his shoulders.

“Whoowee!” Deputy Quinton whooped like a kid on Christmas morning getting an unexpectedly cool present. “This bastard is worse than the others, ain't it boss?”

“What does he mean by the others?” Mchutson asked.

It was his cow and his land. Perry Mchutson was a cranky old fart at the best of times. Today he was riled up from the death of his cow. That sure didn't make him any friendlier.

"Now hold on, Perry," Sheriff Amos said.

"You mean to tell me this. . ." Mchutson raged, "whatever the hell this is has happened to other folks around here!"

"Sure has," Deputy Quinton answered before Sheriff Amos could, with far too much excitement in his voice. Sheriff Amos made a mental note for the hundredth time in his career to fire the hyper, little fool. "That one there is the fourth this week."

"Holy hellfire, Sheriff," Mchutson gawked at him. "What the devil is going on and why ain't you done something about it already?"

"I'll admit there's some animal out there that's having a heyday with the cattle around these parts," Sheriff Amos kept his voice calm and expression professional. "That's all I can tell you, Perry. Nobody has gotten a look at the thing."

"You an idiot too like your deputy over there, Amos?" Mchutson pointed at the tracks near the dead cow. "You do see those, don't ya?"

"I do," Sheriff Amos admitted guardedly.

"They around all the other dead cows too?" Mchutson pressed.

Sheriff Amos sighed. "Yeah, they are, Perry."

"Then you damn well know what you're dealing with, don't ya, Sheriff?" Mchutson took a step towards him but thought better of it, backing off.

"What you're thinking isn't possible," Sheriff Amos did sigh loudly now.

"What's that supposed to mean?" Mchutson spat. "You saying those tracks ain't real, like a hoax or something?"

"Or something," Sheriff Amos said sternly.

Mchutson removed his hat and reached up to scratch at his balding head.

"Don't you worry, sir," Deputy Quinton piped up again. "Whatever is out there you can bet we're gonna get it and put an end to these killings."

The expression on Mchutson's face could only be described as skeptical. He looked back over at Amos. "You see that you do, Sheriff. You got me?"

"I got ya," Sheriff Amos nodded.

The farmer turned to walk away towards his house but Sheriff Amos called after him, "Perry, I'm gonna need to have Doc Thomas come up and take a look at this body. I'd rather you not shoot him."

“If he can help you get whatever's out there, Sheriff, and stop it before I lose another head of cattle, he's welcome here,” Mchutson shouted and then disappeared into the house. The screen door slammed loudly in his wake.

“Pretty happy camper, ain't he?” Deputy Quinton said too loudly for Sheriff Amos' liking.

“Will you shut up already?” Sheriff Amos' eyes shot daggers at the little deputy.

Seeing the level of anger that was seething in Amos, Quinton swallowed hard and then croaked, “Yes sir.”

“Come on,” Sheriff Amos motioned for Quinton to follow him to their patrol car. The two of them had rode out together. One never knew exactly how things were going to go with Perry Mchutson and it was better to have backup on hand in case the situation took a downward turn. Thankfully, today, it hadn't despite the cranky old bastard's loss.

“You really don't believe in Bigfoot, huh?” Quinton challenged him out of the blue.

“What the hell are you babbling about now?” Sheriff Amos snapped.

“Those tracks. . .they've been at all the scenes, Sheriff,” Quinton reminded him. “Ain't nothing else I know of that could have made them."

"Since when did you become a leading cryptozoologist, Quinton?" Sheriff Amos shot back.

"A Crypt-what, boss?" Quinton stuttered.

"Forget it," Sheriff Amos sighed.

"It's gotta be a Bigfoot," Quinton went on. "It's just gotta be."

"No. It doesn't," Sheriff Amos opened the driver's side door and got behind the wheel and Quinton hurried to get into the passenger side. "Anybody with the right skill set could concoct those tracks, make them up to look real."

"So are we not going to make casts of these like the other ones?" Quinton asked.

"What's the point? We got three sets already, don't we?" Sheriff Amos cranked up the patrol car and thrust it into reverse, backing out of the drive onto the main road below it. "What we need is someone who knows about this kind of crap."

"We could always call in Packard on this one," Quinton suggested.

"That guy is a nutjob and you know it, Quinton," Sheriff Amos scowled and his grip on the steering wheel tightened. "And I am not that desperate. . .yet."

"What are we going to do then, Sheriff?" Quinton was staring across the car at him.

"I don't know," Sheriff Amos said, "but for now, we're gonna keep our eyes open and ears to the ground. You can bet on that."

Sheriff Amos knew he was going to have to come up with a hell of a lot better plan than what he had just told Quinton and fragging fast too.

****

There were no stars in the sky. The night was black except for the pale moon. The beast was trapped. William watched the Sasquatch inside the massive metal cage that he and his men had managed to drop upon it. They would have never been able to do so without Nasi's elephant gun. Whereas the beast shrugged off the bullets Henry, Albert, and himself fired into it, Nasi's huge gun had nearly blown the beast's right leg from its body. The leg was so badly damaged, the beast hobbled about barely able to put any weight on it, moving from one side of the cage to another, pounding upon the steel bars.

William noticed Nasi staring worriedly at the cage.

"Don't worry, old friend," William said, "The

cage will hold."

"It best had," Nasi growled, reloading his weapon. "That thing gets out. . ."

"It won't," William assured him.

Henry and Albert were lugging a barrel of oil from the woods. The group had hidden it away near the cage trap that they had lured the beast into.

"Are you sure you want to do this?" Nasi looked at William, frowning.

"That thing. . ." William gritted his teeth, "It killed my family, Nasi. I will have my vengeance as is my right."

Nasi nodded and said nothing more. Turning, Nasi motioned for their companions to hurry up. Henry and Albert positioned the barrel so that it could be dumped into the cage and emptied it there. Oil splashed over and across the dry grass beneath the Sasquatch's feet.

Henry and Albert lit a pair of torches and approached William, offering him one. He accepted it.

Then it was William who moved forward. Henry, Albert, and Nasi watched as he walked up to the cage, standing just beyond the Sasquatch's reach as the beast shoved a hair-covered, thickly-muscled arm between the bars, trying to grab him.

"Blood for blood, you bastard," William said to the beast. "May you forever burn in Hell."

William touched the torch to the oil-soaked grass and hurled himself backwards as the grass within the cage went up in an explosive flash. The heat was so intense his own clothes nearly caught fire.

Inside the cage, the Sasquatch wailed and thrashed about as flames roared up its body. The hair covering it caught and burned. The beast threw itself into the bars of the cage. They shook from the impact, bending slightly outward. The beast lacked the strength to heave itself into them again or they may have broken. Heat came out through the bars in waves. William smiled as the Sasquatch's leg gave way and its already damaged bone finally completely snapped with a sharp crack. Collapsing onto the burning grass, the beast rolled back and forth, shrieking and crying. Cooked layers of flesh sloughed from its bones. Fat bubbled and popped, its cheeks swelling and shrinking back down only to rise again. Its black lips sizzled against yellow teeth. The Sasquatch's cries rose in pitch and volume, foaming spittle flying from its lips before they began to subside into a pained whimpering. Dragging itself back over to the bars, its burning hands clutched them. The beast raised its head. William met the thing's gaze without flinching. Inside, he felt nothing but a cold hollowness, not the pleasure he had expected to. Nonetheless, he took comfort in seeing justice done. Emily and Sarah could rest in peace now. Their killer had been caught and punished.

Nasi stepped forward, raising his elephant gun to put the beast out of its misery.

"No," William said firmly, slapping the weapon's barrel down. "Let the creature burn."

Clearly disapproving of his choice, Nasi glared at him but obeyed. Henry and Albert remained where they were, silent, afraid to do anything else but stand and watch the beast burn.

The Sasquatch let out a final moan before the flames took its eyes, their lids already burned away. They bulged in their sockets, swelling outward, before bursting from the heated pressure within them. The beast's head thudded to the ground and its body stopped moving.

It was at that moment, Robbie jerked awake in his seat. He rocked forward. The movement sent his tablet crashing to the floor of the classroom. The legs of his chair screeched as it shifted beneath the force of his movement. In the wake of the noise caused by his shattering tablet, the classroom was silent for the span of a heartbeat then erupted into fierce laughter as the other students realized what had happened. Robbie had fallen asleep during class and had just made quite the fool out of himself.

"Quiet!" Mrs. Neal yelled and hurried over to him to ask, "Are you okay, Robert?"

Nodding solemnly, Robbie shook his head to clear it. "Yes ma'am. I guess I just didn't get enough sleep last night."

"Uh huh," Mrs. Neal frowned. "And you likely won't tonight either. I want a three page essay about everything we've covered in class this afternoon on my desk tomorrow."

Great, Robbie thought, like he had needed anything else to go wrong today.

"Yes ma'am," he agreed to the punishment as the bell rang.

Everyone else darted out of the class as quickly as they could but Robbie sat where he was for a second longer. The horror of his dream had shaken him and he wasn't sure his legs would be steady enough to walk on yet.

Alison appeared at his side as if from out of nowhere. She sat two rows behind him in the class and he hadn't seen her coming.

"I think we need to go somewhere we can have a talk," Alison told him. Her tone made sure to let him know she wasn't just making a suggestion. Alison wasn't going to let him get away until she knew what was going on with him. Robbie could see that in her eyes.

Overhearing Alison, Mrs. Neal chimed in, "See if you can talk some sense into him while you have him."

Alison chuckled. "I'll certainly do my best, ma'am."

Robbie let her help him get out of his chair and onto his feet. He followed her out of the classroom. This time, the dream had been different than those he normally had about the monster that stalked his nightmares. It hadn't felt the same. Instead of feeling as if he was with the monster in real time, this daydream that had helped further damage his social standing in the school, he was sure of that, felt more like something. . .old. That was the best way he could describe it at any rate. As if he had been watching an old movie instead of living the events of the dream alongside the beast...not that it had been any less disturbing or terrifying.

"Rob," Alison said, her voice oozing with frustration. "Are you listening to me?"

Robbie's attention snapped onto her in laser

focus. “What? No. I'm sorry.”

Alison's eyes cut into him. Her expression wasn't exactly angry though. There was more than a touch of pity in them and that was way worse.

“You're having bad dreams again, aren't you?” she asked.

“I wasn't aware they ever stopped,” Robbie responded more snidely than he meant to.

It was Alison's turn to look hurt.

“Rob, I'm just trying to be a good friend here,” she frowned, “I'm worried about you.”

“I know,” Robbie almost whispered, ashamed of himself.

The bleachers that stood around and above the football field were empty. No one was using the field or track for practice this afternoon. Alison led them to the top of the bleachers and took a seat, patting the spot next to her. With a heavy sigh, Robbie shrugged off his backpack, placing it in front of him, as he sat where she indicated.

“Look,” Robbie went for broke trying to get things over with as quick as he could, like ripping away a Band-Aid. “The dreams are bad. I mean real bad.”

"You wanna talk about them?" Alison asked, though it was clear she wanted him to.

Robbie sucked in a deep breath. "They're about a monster. . .only it isn't always the same monster or at least doesn't seem to be."

"A monster?" Alison asked, a bit disbelieving.

"Yeah, a monster," Robbie nodded.

"Like a demon?" Alison reached over to take one of his hands. Robbie pulled it away.

"No, not a demon," Robbie told her firmly. "A monster."

"I don't understand," Alison stared at him, waiting for him to go on.

"You won't believe me," Robbie met her eyes.

"I'm not going to laugh at you if that's what you're worried about," she assured him.

"It's Bigfoot, okay?" Robbie regretted naming the beast aloud as soon as the words were out of his mouth. It felt like uttering a curse or spell that would bring the creature to him in real life.

He watched her face contort in a grimace as she fought to control herself and not laugh. Alison didn't dare say anything for fear of losing it.

“I'm not joking, Alison,” Robbie told her. “I keep seeing this huge, hairy monster in my dreams. I watch it tear people apart. Last night, I was along for the ride as it killed a bunch of hunters up on Harold Mountain. It ate them, Alison. Right in front of my eyes and there wasn't a damn thing I could do about it.”

Alison didn't say a word. Robbie didn't know if she was in shock from what he'd told her or if she thought he was so crazy that she didn't know what to say.

Robbie reached over to take her hands this time. “I'm really fragging crazy, aren't I? I . . .I'm sorry. You asked me to tell you the truth. Well everything I just told you. . .it's the truth.”

As if coming out of a trance, Alison shook her head.

“No. No, it's okay, Robbie,” she stammered, “I am glad you told me.”

She placed the palm of her right hand on his cheek, holding it there.

“Me too,” he smiled, relaxing more than he would have thought possible. “Somehow it makes everything a bit easier just to have been able to tell someone else about the nightmares.”

“I guess the question is what are we gonna do

about these nightmares of yours?" Alison's lips curled downward in a frown.

"If I knew what to do about them," Robbie leaned forward to touch his forehead to hers, "I'd be rid of them already."

Gently pulling away, Alison met his eyes again. "No one else knows?"

"Not a soul," Robbie assured her.

"And that was what happened to you in class today?" Alison had to have known the answer before asking him but she did anyway.

"That class is so boring and since I haven't really been sleeping. . .I nodded off. The next thing I knew I was having another daymare, if you want to call it that," Robbie confirmed.

"It sure looked intense," Alison commented.

"It was," Robbie agreed, "But it wasn't like the nightmares I normally have at night. It was different."

"How?" Alison pressed him. "What made it different? The level of intensity?"

"Nope. All of them are that bad. This daymare though, it was different because I wasn't seeing things directly through the monster's eyes. It was more like reliving something that happened in the past, bearing witness to it. A group of men, hunters I think, had trapped the monster in a metal cage. It wasn't able to kill any of them."

"Then what made the daymare so bad?"

"They burnt the monster alive," Robbie explained. "They doused it in some kind of oil and set it on fire. I watched it burn, Alison. Every terrible, nauseating moment of the thing's death."

Alison covered her mouth in astonishment and horror. "Oh Rob, I am so sorry."

They sat for a second in silence before either of them spoke again.

"What I don't understand," Alison finally said, "is why was this daymare different? It doesn't make sense for you to be seeing through the monster's eyes in all the others but then not in this one."

"I don't have an answer to that, Alison," Robbie's shoulders slumped from a mixture of exhaustion and frustration. "I really don't."

Having had their heart to heart like she wanted, Alison was content to drop all of it for now as both of them needed to get home. Well, he really didn't need to. His parents were in another country after all but he went along with it being late so that he could walk with her.

They left the school grounds and turned eastward, strolling up Evergreen Street. Her parents' house was even closer to the school than his was.

Robbie nearly jumped out of his skin as a sheriff car with its siren wailing blew past them. It quickly vanished over the slight hill ahead of them. Mere seconds later, another patrol car blared by them in its wake.

“What the. . .?” Robbie gasped. Clyde was a quiet, peaceful town, the sort of postcard picture perfect place that folks got nostalgic about.

“Maybe they're headed to a wreck,” Alison offered in way of an explanation.

“Sheriffs don't normally handle that kind of thing,” Robbie pointed out. “That's more of a police or highway patrol thing.”

Alison didn't look convinced and she had a point. Clyde didn't have a police department of its own. The closest was in Pisgah, the next town over.

“Hey!” they heard Warren's voice calling out to them. He was running up the street towards them.

Robbie and Alison stood where they were, letting him catch up to them.

Warren looked from one of them to the other.

"You guys haven't heard, have you?"

"Heard what?" Robbie barked, not in the mood for Warren's usual crap after having such a heavy talk with Alison.

"Susie Mullens is missing, buddy," Warren blurted out.

"What?" Alison wailed and then she was gone, running on up the hill.

Warren watched her go.

"I guess she knew the kid, huh?" Warren fished a cigarette and lighter from his pocket, firing up.

Robbie slapped the cigarette out of his hand.

"Of course she knew her, you idiot!" Robbie snarled. "She's been babysitting her for like two years now. You've even met her before."

Warren blinked in disbelief at what Robbie had done. "How the hell was I supposed to know that, huh?"

Shaking his head and barely controlling the anger flaring up within him, Robbie kept himself from punching Warren. "You're Alison's friend too, aren't you? Don't you ever listen to anything she's saying?"

"Kind of," Warren answered honestly. "I mean she's hot but man she's boring as hell too."

Robbie started to take off after Alison but Warren stopped him.

“Don't you wanna know what happened?” Warren asked.

Hating himself for it, Robbie paused to let Warren talk. As messed up as Warren's stories sometimes were, Robbie figured he'd get more out of him than the police. They sure as hell weren't going to stop and let a kid like him in on everything that was going on.

“They say that she was out in the woods behind her house playing last night and never came home,” Warren got out another cigarette and lit it, taking a long drag before continuing. “Her parents hunted for her all night. It wasn't until this morning that they called the cops, if you can buy that, because the girl has a treehouse or a fort or something out there that she would sleep in from time to time during the summer. Personally, I think they murdered her themselves and are just trying to cover it up. Ain't that how it usually goes down on those crime shows?”

“That doesn't explain why those cops went flying that way right now, Warren,” Robbie challenged him.

“Oh yeah,” Warren seemed to realize he had in fact forgotten to tell part of what he knew.

"That. . .Well, you see, according to the rumor mill, they just found part of her dress in the woods, all torn up with blood on it. That got the cops taking things a lot more seriously all of a sudden I guess."

Warren was staring at him. "You look like you know something too, man? Fair's fair, ya know?"

"Not now," Robbie didn't waste any more time. He ran up the hill too, wanting to be there for Alison like she had just been for him.

****

Sheriff Amos was the last officer to arrive on the scene. All of his deputies except for Henreitta, who was assigned to dispatch, were already there. It was a fact he instantly came to regret. Jacob Mullens was on him as soon as he'd gotten out of his patrol car. Mullens came at him hard. He couldn't blame the man. If he had a twelve year old daughter that was missing, Amos knew he would be in the same sort of state that Jacob was.

"Where in the hell have you been, Amos?" Jacob spat at him.

Jacob's arms shot out in an attempt to shove him up against the side of his patrol car. Amos caught them easily, being careful not to do too much damage as he used Jacob's own momentum to swing the shorter man into the car and hold him there.

"Easy there, Jacob," Amos warned. "I came as soon as I could."

That was a lie but Amos ran with it. He'd assigned the handling of Susie being missing to his best deputy, Bethany Rogers, knowing that she could handle it. It wasn't like Clyde was a town crawling with child abductors or serial killers and even if it were, he'd still have had faith in Rogers.

"She's gone, Amos!" Jacob struggled, trying to get loose. "My little girl is gone!"

Amos noticed that Ryan and Michelle, two EMTS, were on the scene as well, their ambulance parked closer to the Mullens' house.

"Ryan!" Amos called out. "Get this man a sedative before I have to arrest him for assaulting an officer."

The two EMTS came running after Michelle reached into the rear of the ambulance to grab a kit. Sheriff Amos kept Jacob where he was, trying to keep the man from hurting him or himself until they got there. Michelle plunged a syringe into Jacob. Jacob stopped thrashing about and went limp in Amos' arms.

“Help him,” Sheriff Amos ordered Ryan and Michelle.

“You got it, Sheriff,” Ryan said as they took Jacob off his hands.

Unlike her husband, Sherri Mullens wasn't raging about. Sherri stood on the house's porch, gaze locked onto the woods beyond it, almost as if she were in a trance. Deputy Rogers was with her. Amos could see the strain on Bethany's face. She'd been dealing with this mess since the early morning and the discovery of the torn and bloody dress was certainly a development that no one had seen coming. Things like this just didn't happen in Clyde.

As he came up the short set of steps to the house's porch, Amos gave Bethany a look that let her know that he would be taking over.

“It's going to be okay, ma'am. Sheriff Amos is here now,” Bethany patted Sherri gently on the back and then headed down the steps to get out of his way.

Sherri didn't seem to hear Bethany at all. That worried Amos. He'd almost rather have had her come at him like her husband did.

“Mrs. Mullens,” Sheriff Amos addressed her. “We're doing everything we can to find Susie. Don't let what we've found so far take away all your hope. She could have just cut herself out there or taken a fall. There's no reason to assume the worst."

Sherri's head swiveled around slowly; her hollow, hurt-filled eyes fell on him. She sucked in a sharp breath as if realizing he was there for the first time.

"Sherri? Did you hear what I said?" Amos asked.

"She's not coming home, Sheriff," Sherri told him.

"Now, we don't know that. . ." Amos began but she cut him off.

"I can feel it in my bones. A mother just knows these things," Sherri trembled as she spoke.

"Well. . ." Sheriff Amos did his best to find the right words to say, "Like I said, we're going to do everything we can to bring her home."

He'd wanted to ask her some questions about the night before and Susie but could see that Sherri was too far gone in her grief for him to even try. His gut told him that he wouldn't get anywhere if he did.

Deputy Rogers was waiting for him at the corner of the house.

“Whew, sorry I dumped all this on you, Bethany,” Sheriff Amos walked up to her.

“It's the job,” her voice was flat.

“So fill me in,” Sheriff Amos ordered, “What do we know?”

“Honestly, not much,” Bethany frowned. “From what I've put together, everything was completely normal last night. No fights in the family, nothing odd, it was just another evening. They had dinner and little Susie went out to play like she does most nights. Sherri made her take a jacket since the nights are getting colder now, told her not to stay out too long. Still, apparently neither of them worried until after nine. When she hadn't come back, they panicked and instead of calling us, rushed into the woods themselves. They went to her fort, or whatever you want to call it, but Susie wasn't there, then spent the night out there running around with flashlights and shouting for her. It was around 3 AM when they gave up and came home to call us. As you know, I was first on the scene around 3:30.”

“You went out there yourself?” Sheriff Amos gestured towards the nearby trees.

“I did,” Bethany nodded. “I figured out real quick that I wasn't going to find the little girl on my own so I came back and called in help. By dawn, just about everyone was out here with me except for you, Quinton and Dispatch. It wasn't until we found the piece of Susie's dress that I called in Ryan and Michelle. And as you can see, just about everyone on the street is around watching things play out."

"Sounds like you handled things better than most would have," Sheriff Amos complimented her.

"Thanks," Bethany managed a weak grin.

"Take me to where you found the dress," Sheriff Amos motioned for her to lead him into the woods and then followed her in.

"It was just blind luck we found the dress at all," Bethany told him. "The spot where it was is far away from the girl's fort."

The walk into the woods was indeed a lot longer than he would have expected. The two of them passed the girl's small "lean to" style house and kept going north towards Harold Mountain. Why the girl would have gone on so far on her own, Sheriff Amos couldn't come up with any reason for. He kept alert, taking in everything around them that he could but nothing really seemed out of place.

Finally, Bethany stopped. "This is where we found it."

She pointed at the ground. “Right there.”

Sheriff Amos knelt to examine the ground. There were no signs of a struggle or even tracks at the spot that Bethany indicated.

“Nothing there, right?” Bethany asked.

He shook his head. “Why do I feel like you're about to make me regret getting into law enforcement again?”

“Because you'd be right,” Bethany chuckled darkly. “No tracks or anything else where we found the dress but follow me. . .”

Bethany led him a few yards to the west. Sheriff Amos saw what she was taking him to before they reached it. “Bloody fragging hell!”

Sheriff Amos spotted not just the tracks but the path that was torn through the woods easily. Something huge had clearly walked away in the direction of Harold Mountain and the tracks it left behind were deep. The thing had to be as heavy as it was large. There was blood on the ground too.

Taking a moment to regain his composure, Sheriff Amos really wished he still smoked. His nerves were like frayed wircs. He was on edge and knew it.

“You okay?” Bethany was staring at him.

“No,” he answered honestly. “I'm not. Either I'm losing my mind or we have a freaking monster living in the woods around these parts.”

“You know what Sherlock Holmes always said,” Bethany said. “When you have eliminated then. . .”

“Yeah, I get it, Beth. I do,” Sheriff Amos glared at her. There was just too much evidence to argue with at this point, or at least he was beginning to feel that way.

“These are the same types of tracks that we've been finding with the mutilated cattle,” Bethany frowned.

“We don't know that the girl's dead,” Sheriff Amos challenged what he assumed Bethany had already concluded.

“Again, the evidence. . .” Bethany was cut short.

“Let's not just jump to that,” Sheriff Amos barked.

Bethany shrugged and raised her hands in a gesture of surrender. “I'll admit we don't have a body.”

“But we do have a trail,” Sheriff Amos looked around. “It's possible that the beast or whatever the hell it is was carrying the girl off and part of her dress was torn away and just got moved by the wind to where we found it."

Sheriff Amos was stretching things to an absurd length but that didn't mean what he said wasn't plausible. He didn't want to think about the little girl being ripped apart and eaten like the cattle had been.

"Oh no," Bethany was shaking her head. "Don't tell me you're thinking. . ."

"We need to call in some help and follow these tracks, Deputy," his tone switched to being cold and very professional.

****

Robbie unlocked the side door and hurried inside. He flung his backpack roughly onto the kitchen table. Hurrying to the fridge, Robbie yanked it open, grabbing an energy drink from within it. He chugged half the can before finally lowering it from his lips. Alison had been wrecked by Susie's disappearance. She had cried and cried and cried, wailing in his arms. The deputies keeping the crowd away from the Mullens' house, including the two of them, hadn't said anything about the little girl being dead but that was sure what Alison seemed to think. Comforting her had been nigh impossible. Robbie wasn't good at that sort of emotional stuff anyway and trying so hard for her had pushed him to, maybe, beyond the limit of what he could handle.

Plopping down into a seat at the table, Robbie set down his energy drink and reached up to rub his temples. His head was throbbing. Robbie wondered if he should still be there with Alison right now. Her parents had come home though and she'd left with them. Robbie supposed he could have gone with them. Her mom and dad both thought highly of him. They likely wouldn't have protested if he had tried. Maybe they would have even welcomed the additional help dealing with the breakdown Alison appeared to be having. He hadn't realized just how close Alison and Susie apparently had become. If he was honest with himself though, Robbie knew that getting the hell out of there was the best thing and was glad he'd done it.

Robbie looked at his hands. They were trembling. The energy drink only made things worse. He'd thought it would help clear his head but that hadn't happened. His thoughts were even more muddled now than before. Things like this didn't happen in real life except on the news or in a movie. But it had happened, here in Clyde of all places, and to someone he knew. Swallowing hard, Robbie left the energy drink where it was and went to lock the door he'd come in through before heading upstairs.

The house felt empty and far too big to be alone in with his parents away. He considered calling Warren to have him come over but thought better of it. All Warren would do was continue to hassle him about having a party on Friday night. Warren was obsessed with the idea, truly believing it could turn them from social rejects into part of the cool crowd. Robbie suffered from no such delusion. Even if the party was a hit, they might be cool for a night, maybe even a few days, but with time, sooner rather than later, people would forget and they would be the same rejects they had always been.

One glance at his bed and Robbie shuddered. As if the real world wasn't bad enough, there would be fresh and darker horrors waiting for him when he lay down and closed his eyes. Robbie was emotionally drained but the energy drink he had chugged half of was fully kicking in now. He moved to his desk and took a seat in the swivel gaming chair in front of it. Picking up the remote, he clicked on his TV. The local news was on and of course talking about little Susie's disappearance. Robbie's anger at the entire situation flared and he was on the verge of turning the TV back off. What stopped him was the reporter showing an image of a footprint. Kicking up the volume, he watched, attention glued to the screen.

“Tracks like these are reported to have been found in the same area where a torn and bloodied piece of the child's dress was discovered. As you can see, though very similar to a human's in shape, these tracks are far too large and deep to have been left by any man.”

Robbie's eyes widened. No, he thought, it can't be.

“As many of our viewers are likely already thinking, yes, it's very possible that these tracks belong to a Bigfoot or a Sasquatch. Again, there is no hard evidence that this is the case but. . .that is what they appear to be. Our investigative team has done some digging and discovered that these tracks here at the scene of the girl's disappearance are not the only tracks of this sort to be found in Clyde in recent weeks. Before little Susie went missing, several farmers reported the bizarre mutilation of their cattle. When asked for comment if there is any connection between the mauling of the cattle and this missing child, the Clyde Sheriff Department declined to comment.”

The shot cut away to an anchorwoman at the main news desk. “Thanks for that first hand report, Geddy,” the anchorwoman purred. “Despite the lack of clear evidence, as you can see,” the shot changed again to show the parking lot outside of a local hotel where dozens of tough looking, rough men were unloading hunting gear. “As you can see, word is already getting out about the chance of there being a Bigfoot in the Clyde area. Hunters and trackers are pouring in from all over.”

Realizing his hands had come up to steeple over his mouth as if silencing a gasp he lowered them, gaze still fixed on the screen. He hadn't known anything about the cattle killings but that they had happened made sense if the monster in his nightmares was real and actually out there. Surely it couldn't be, could it? The news didn't mention anything about the group of hunters he'd seen die last night in his dreams. Had they just not been found yet or was he losing his mind in considering that the thing in his dreams might be real?

Robbie spun around in his chair and fired up his desktop. His fingers typed the word nightmares in his search bar and he punched enter. The screen was instantly filled with tons of sites. He scrolled through looking for causes, cures, and most of all at sites that dealt with clairvoyant and precognitive/post-cognitive dreams. He needed to understand what was happening to him, what his dreams meant. He just had to.

****

Sheriff Amos smashed a fist down into the top of the table his deputies were gathered around. “Damn it to hell! Anyone want to tell me just how the press got wind of the tracks we've been finding?”

“Somebody had to have leaked them,” Bethany spoke up. “It's the only explanation.”

Looking around the table, Sheriff Amos eyed his people. Quinton was playing with a pencil, barely tuned into the conversation. Bethany, he trusted fully so his gaze quickly moved on from her. Henreitta was the same. It was unlikely she'd let anything slip. His focus lingered for a heartbeat on Harry. The overweight, nearly bald deputy had given him some trouble in the last two years but didn't seem dumb enough to do something this sketchy. His buddy, Benji, was at the top of Amos' list of suspects. Younger and more in shape than Harry but lacking the older man's experience at making the job work for him instead of him working for the people of Clyde, Amos could easily see him selling the info to the press. Even if Benji had, Amos didn't think he'd ever get the proof to bust him for it. Hicks and Adams finished out his group of deputies. Both of them were rock solid guys. He knew Adams was having a lot of issues at home right now and was well aware how things like that could mess with someone in their line of work.

“Y'all better pray I never find out who did this,” Sheriff Amos swore. “And it damn well better not happen again. Do I make myself clear?”

Everyone at the table either answered with a prompt “yes sir” or nodded.

“We will be coming back to this, I can promise you that, but for right now, we've got bigger things to deal with,” Sheriff Amos snarled. “Our little town is about to be Bigfoot hunter central! We're gonna have more armed A holes than we can count all over the place. Not to mention Susie Mullens is still missing.”

“Should we be calling in some help from Asheville or Canton?” Henreitta asked.

Sheriff Amos shook his head. “Not yet. We've got enough outsiders in town already. Calling in more might just be adding more fuel to the fire instead of helping to keep it under control.”

“What do we do then?” Harry challenged him. “Start going around asking all these self proclaimed Bigfoot hunters for their gun permits?”

"That sounds like a good idea to me," Hicks leaned forward, more than happy to go risk a bunch of altercations in order to get the job done. Sheriff Amos knew he couldn't let him do that though. The hunters were going to greatly outnumber them. Even with the law on their side and guns on their hips, there was no point in going looking for trouble if it could be helped. And he thought it could be for now. That could change if the hunters started getting rowdy around town but he was hoping that wouldn't happen as they should be spending the majority of their time out in the woods.

"No," Sheriff Amos told Hicks. "I think our best bet is just to try and keep an eye on things and deal with problems one on one as they come up. That's what most of us will be doing. Bethany, I want you, Quinton, and Benji to get back to hunting for the Mullens girl. Give Stiles a call. I want her and her dogs out here pronto. Use them to find Susie before these outsiders do."

"I'll do my best," Bethany assured him.

He could see that she understood why he had saddled her with Quinton and Benji. The two of them he couldn't trust not to cause trouble with the hunters but out there with her, they'd at least be extra sets of eyes and ears.

"Adams, I want you to take charge in town," Sheriff Amos ordered. "Everybody not with Bethany, you're with him."

"What are you going to be doing, Sheriff?" Adams asked.

"There's one of these hunters in particular I want to pay a visit to myself," Sheriff Amos picked up his hat from the table and put it on. "So let's get to it, people."

The meeting broke up. Sheriff Amos had kept it as short as he could. He briskly stomped through the department and out into the parking lot. His people knew what to do and he trusted them to get it done. Slinging open the door to his personal patrol car, he slid into it and cranked up. Shifting the car into reverse and backing out of his space, Sheriff Amos headed for the local Motel 6. The gentleman, if the guy could be called that, went by the name of Blackburn. He was supposed to be one of the leading cryptozoologists in the United States. Blackburn was a well established and famous big game hunter. The guy had no criminal record and based on what Sheriff Amos could find out about him, Blackburn always conducted himself as a professional. The man himself wasn't a problem but his fans sure as hell could be. Sheriff Amos hoped to speak with

Blackburn. If he could get him on his side and helping to control the other hunters it would help a lot.

Sheriff Amos parked outside the Motel 6's guest entrance and went inside. Andy, the main day shift clerk, was behind the desk.

"How you doing, Sheriff?" Andy asked, putting on a smile, though there was a clear tone of worry in his voice. Sheriff Amos had served a good number of warrants at the hotel over the years. "Anything up I should be concerned about?"

"Not today, Andy," Sheriff Amos said and saw Andy visibly relax. "I just need to speak with one of your guests."

"Okay," Andy's worry returned to his face. "And who would that be?"

"Staker Blackburn," Sheriff Amos answered.

Andy flinched behind his desk.

"I don't care if you call him down here or just give me his room number, Andy. Really, the guy's not in any sort of trouble. I only want to talk to him."

"He's on the first floor. Demanded a room down here. You can find him through those doors in room five, third one on the right."

“Thanks, Andy,” Sheriff Amos gave the clerk an appreciative nod.

“No need to come huntin' for me, Sheriff,” a deep voice sounded behind him before he could turn around. When he did, Blackburn was standing in the lobby only a few feet away.

“Mr. Blackburn?” Sheriff Amos ventured.

“That's me,” Blackburn grinned. “What can I do for you? You come to check out my gun permits?”

Sheriff Amos could tell that the hunter was joking and couldn't help liking him. The guy seemed to have a talent at putting folks at ease.

“No, nothing like that,” Sheriff Amos matched his smile. “I'm actually here just to ask a favor.”

“Tell ya what then, Sheriff, why don't we step on outside and talk about it,” Blackburn offered.

As soon as they were through the front doors, Blackburn plopped a thick cigar in his mouth and lit up.

“Mr. Blackburn,” Sheriff Amos began but Blackburn was ahead of him.

“I know why you're here and I'll do what I can to keep the amateurs in line,” Blackburn told him.

Sheriff Amos was impressed by the lean hunter. “Thanks. With everything going on in this town, I need all the help I can get.”

Blackburn puffed on his cigar. “No problem at all, Sheriff. The less chaos there is, the better for all of us. I don't need it getting in my way either.”

“You really think there's a Sasquatch out there in the woods somewhere?” Sheriff Amos asked.

“Don't you?” Blackburn challenged him. “From what I've heard, you've seen plenty of evidence of just that.”

“More than I'd like, that's for sure,” Sheriff Amos frowned.

“Most folks usually have a really hard time accepting the existence of cryptids at first,” Blackburn told him. “If they live long enough, they tend to come around though.”

“Live long enough?” Sheriff Amos cocked an eyebrow.

“Yep,” Blackburn said, “The crypto world, well most of it, has Bigfoot all wrong, Sheriff. He ain't no peaceful giant. I can straight up tell you that. Most Sasquatch will leave you alone as long as you stay out of their turf but you step into it and you could very quickly and easily end up dead. And some Sasquatch, they get a taste for violence and blood, Sheriff. They're the ones you really have to watch out for and that's what I think you have here, a beast that's got some serious anger issues."

Sheriff Amos grunted. "Can't say I am happy to hear that."

"Don't you worry about the Sasquatch, Sheriff," Blackburn smirked, "My boys and I will deal with it."

"There's a little girl missing out there, ya know?" Sheriff Amos informed Blackburn.

"I heard." Blackburn ground out what was left of his cigar in the ashtray can just outside the Motel 6 entrance. "I'm sorry about that. Odds are she's long dead. Best if you accept that, Sheriff."

"I can't do that," Sheriff Amos shook his head. "Her parents are counting on me to bring her home."

"Then if I come across her body out there, Sheriff, I'll give you a call," Blackburn said. "See ya around, brother."

Blackburn disappeared back into the Motel 6, taking what remained of his cigar with him.

Sheriff Amos' gut told him he could trust the guy and that Blackburn would do as he said in helping control the other hunters and cryptid groupies who had invaded the town.

****

Bethany, Quinton, and Benji stood outside the Mullens' house. The trio of deputies watched as Stiles' pickup pulled up to the curb. Quinton whistled as Wanda Stiles got out. Bethany elbowed him so hard that he almost lost his balance. Quinton whirled on her, cheeks red with rage, but as soon as he saw her fierce scowl, he threw his arms up and simply said, "What the hell?"

"Shut up, Quinton," Benji snapped. "Nobody's got time for your crap right now."

Shoulders slumping like a scolded child, Quinten was frowning as Stiles loosed her dogs from the rear of the covered pickup. He kicked at a small rock at the edge of the street, eyes turned downward. They did cut upwards every so often though to steal a glance of Stiles. The dog handler was the closest thing the little town of Clyde had to a fully bonafide supermodel. Stiles was lean but still curvy in the right places as men saw things. Her long blonde hair was pulled back roughly into a ponytail. Stiles' legs were long and her waist tiny. The woman had deep, blue eyes but usually, like today, they remained hidden behind thick, dark sunglasses.

"Stiles," Bethany gave the dog handler a nod of acknowledgement, walking up to meet her. "Good to see you again."

"You too, Deputy, though the circumstances could certainly be better," Stiles frowned. "Think there's any hope of us finding this girl alive?"

Bethany shrugged, "I honestly have no clue. I'd wager it's not likely."

"Well. . ." Stiles said, "If anyone can find her, it's my boys here. There's not a lot of daylight left. You sure you want to do this right now, though?"

Bethany nodded. "No choice. Every second counts, you know that."

Wally, Ruger, and Manstopper sat peacefully now that they were out of the truck. The three dogs were all German Shepards and large for their breed. Bethany had seen Stiles pull off miracles with them before.

"Best get to it then," Bethany handed Stiles a small, stuffed doll which had been crammed into her jacket pocket. "This was the girl's."

Stiles accepted the doll, happy to have it. She used it to give the dogs the girl's scent then led the way into the woods beyond the Mullens' house. Bethany and the other deputies paused long enough to arm up and then followed after her. Benji took a pump action twelve gauge from his patrol car. Bethany handed Quinton an AR-15 from the trunk of her own and then selected a shotgun like Benji's for herself.

“Damn,” Stiles commented as they caught up to her. “You hunting for a lost girl or going to war? Don't tell me. . .”

“I'm not saying I fully believe the Bigfoot stuff, Wanda,” Bethany told the dog handler, “but I find it's best to be safe instead of sorry.”

“Right,” Stiles stifled a chuckle. “Whatever you say, Beth.”

Bethany was a bit put off by the shortening of her name on such friendly terms when they were out in the field like this.

“I thought these woods would be flooded by Bigfoot hunters already,” Stiles changed the subject. “Those jerks might not be as careful as the three of you will be with their firearms.”

“There are likely some around,” Bethany admitted.

“Most of those bastards are still at their hotels gearing up or waiting on that Blackburn guy to take the lead,” Benji added. “And if any of them show up out here this evening, we'll deal with them. . .however we need to.”

"By the book," Bethany corrected him. "That's how we will handle them, Benji."

He grunted but didn't challenge her on what she had said.

"That's good, the less folks in these woods the better," Stiles commented. "My boys can find the girl regardless but the hunters not being everywhere is sure as heck going to make it easier."

Stiles gave her dogs slack and kept them moving at a pace they could keep up with amid the trees. They quickly reached the spot where the torn and bloody piece of little Susie's dress had been found earlier. The dogs milled about in the spot for a minute or two getting their bearings and then were off again. Bethany noticed straight away that they were headed in the direction of Harold Mountain. She found that somewhat less than comforting.

"You seeing what I'm seeing?" Stiles asked.

"Huh?" Bethany blinked, ashamed at herself for being caught off guard by Stiles.

"The tracks," Stiles pointed at the ground. There was no mistaking them. They were the same huge footprints that the department found at the scenes of all the cattle mutilations. Bethany's breath caught in her throat at the sight of them. She tried not to let Stiles see just how much the tracks bothered her.

"Yeah, I see them," Bethany struggled to say much more calmly than she felt.

"Ain't no denying those are messed up, Beth," Stiles said, "but they don't mean crap. Bigfoot isn't real. Could there be some big, dumb, shoeless redneck killer out here with a penchant for little girls? I'd say that's a lot more likely."

"A big redneck, huh?" Bethany managed a weak smile.

"Sure," Stiles nodded, "Leatherface could easily leave tracks like those if he was out here barefooted. Madman Marz, Victor Crowley, maybe even Jason could too, ya know?"

"You watch too many horror movies," Quinton cut in. "Those things ain't good for you, ma'am. They'll rot your brain."

Stiles laughed out loud. "Why, Deputy, I didn't know you cared?"

Quinton flushed, shutting up instantly. Stiles clearly enjoyed the discomfort she'd caused him.

"Quit it, you two," Benji grumbled. "We need to keep focused, people. We have no idea what the hell is out here."

****

Robbie's eyes hurt and so did his head. His frantic searching online for information on what he was going through proved to be utterly useless. Discerning the usual internet crap from what was true was just too huge of a task. Rocking back in his chair, Robbie sighed and then flopped forward to rest his elbows atop his deck. The throbbing of his temples convinced him that it was time to give up. He shutdown his laptop and closed it. He needed sleep but that was the very last thing he wanted. Robbie knew that almost certainly as soon as he closed his eyes, the dreams, nightmares, would come again.

He was convinced now that the nightmares were indeed a link between himself and some sort of beast. The closest thing he could relate the creature to was a Sasquatch or Bigfoot. It was the only thing that fit. He had always heard though that Sasquatch were peaceful giants. Of course there were plenty of stories that said otherwise. He'd even heard of a series of books in which an army of the Sasquatch wiped out humanity. Still, the crypto-zoological world held with the peaceful claim and played the beasts as misunderstood and hunted things that rarely ever attacked humans and even then those attacks were because of something that humans had done. So if Sasquatch were peaceful, then what the hell was the thing in his nightmares? Had someone done something horrid to it? Was it after some sort of bestial vengeance against mankind? Did Sasquatch get rabies?

Robbie rubbed at his face and yawned. He knew his own body well enough to accept that it had hit the point where energy drinks weren't going to help him anymore. Accepting his defeat, Robbie moved from the chair at his desk to his bed, flopping heavily onto it. The springs creaked beneath him. He lay with his arms out to his sides, his body resembling a cross. The bed was soft and Robbie felt his eyes closing. With a grunt, he opened them, still fighting the sleep that was threatening to wash over him. Knowing it was a pointless battle didn't matter. He would fight against it every second possible. Anything to avoid the horrid images that were coming.

Staring up at the ceiling, Robbie lost the fight. His eyes drooped shut and his mind slipped into the world of dreams. He heard dogs barking in the distance. They were coming closer to wherever he was. There were trees all around him. Robbie was in the woods again but not the same woods he'd been before so far as he could tell.

He certainly wasn't a nature guy. He had played in the woods some as a little kid but had long left that kind of adventuring behind. His attention was drawn back to the dogs. Somehow he smelt their scent through the link he shared with whatever it was that his dream-self seemed to be bound to.

Robbie felt the creature's rage, burning and primal, deep within its soul. A light rain was falling. The earth beneath the creature's feet wasn't yet soaked so Robbie knew the rain had only just started. The creature looked down and through its eyes, Robbie saw the beast's body, powerful muscles under a thick mess of dirty, brown hair. Raising its head again, the beast sniffed the air. The barking of the dogs continued to draw nearer. Throwing its huge form into motion, the beast glided through the woods like a silent apparition. Mindboggling was the only word with which to describe the ease and fluidity of its movement. It seemed impossible that something so large and powerful could be so quiet.

The beast moved away from the dogs at first, easily putting distance between itself and them, then it cut around to flank the canines. The dogs became confused, sensing that something had changed. Now they were no longer the pursuers but the ones being pursued. The trio of dogs broke up, one darting to the east, another to the west. Those two were smart enough to break and run for their lives. Only the largest of the three was determined, or perhaps stupid, enough to stand its ground. The dog stood, legs firm, back braced, snarling as the beast came into its view. A low, rattling growl rose up within the beast as it stepped towards the dog.

Robbie strained to break free of the connection he shared with the beast. To somehow shut his eyes against the horror that came next. He couldn't bear to see and hear it. The dog leaped. The beast snatched it from the air. There was a sickening crack of snapping bones and splattering of blood. The dog's body thudded onto the ground at the beast's feet, still and broken. Robbie felt sick.

The beast stood motionless, blood dripping from its oversized hands, black lips parted in a silent snarl. The dogs were not its only pursuers. It could hear the voices of the people among the trees approaching from the same direction the dogs had. It listened to the voices a moment and then moved deeper into the shadows of trees, blending in among them to wait for them to come to it.

Robbie was helpless. There was no means of warning those heading towards where the beast waited, nothing he could do to save them.

****

The dogs had stopped barking. They had seemed to be hot on the trail of something and then just stopped. Bethany could see that Stiles was freaking out. The handler started to run on ahead of the rest of them but Benji stepped into her path, stopping her.

"Don't," Benji stared at Stiles, letting her know that she wasn't going through or around him.

"We don't know what's out there," Bethany said.

"Hell no we don't," Quinton agreed.

"But my boys. . ." Stiles stammered.

"I didn't say we weren't going after them," Bethany pointed out, "We just need to be careful about it, is all."

Stiles, still frantic, was managing to hold herself in check, if only just barely. She nodded.

"Quinton, I want you on point," Bethany ordered.

"You got it," he assured her.

The three deputies and the handler got moving. The night was dark, even darker since the rain had rolled in. Dark clouds blocked the starlight but some light from the moon was getting through, enough to allow them to continue to function without using flashlights.

Benji worked the pump of his shotgun, chambering a round. Bethany did the same. Quinton clutched his AR-15 in a white-knuckled grip. All of them were creeped out by the sudden silence from the dogs. They made their way slowly in the darkness, leaves crunching under their feet despite their attempts to remain as quiet as possible.

The beast stepped out of the trees between Quinton and Bethany. Stiles screamed at the sight of it. The thing stood at least eight feet tall. Its body was covered in thick, filthy hair. Long arms, like those of an ape, grabbed hold of Quinton even as he spun around to face the beast. He had no chance to use his shotgun. A hairy hand tore it from his grasp and threw the weapon away into the woods. Quinton, wide-eyed, with his bladder releasing itself, gawked at the snarling, black lipped, far too human face that towered above him.

“Get down!” Bethany yelled as she aimed her shotgun at the thing.

Benji had already opened fire. His shotgun boomed, the sound of its fury echoing amid the trees. He missed his target. The blast struck Quinton instead of the hulking beast. The force of it knocked Quinton backwards. He staggered, his chest blown open, red pouring from the wound.

"Useless bastard," Quinton croaked and then collapsed.

The sound of the shotgun launched the beast into motion. It sprang at Bethany. She was ready for it though. Her shotgun boomed as Bethany squeezed its trigger. A heavy slug slammed into the beast, tearing into its guts, an explosion of blood bursting outward as it entered. It was enough to halt the beast's forward motion. The Sasquatch, or whatever the hell it was, looked down at the hole she'd put in its body. Red slicked, purple bits of intestines poked out its stomach. The smell of feces and bodily fluids was rancid and overpowering. Bethany gagged, breathing it in but stopped herself from vomiting. Chambering another round, she pressed her momentary advantage from the Sasquatch being stunned by the pain she had inflicted upon it. She took aim again just as the Sasquatch recovered. With a thunderous roar, the Sasquatch lunged for her. Bethany fired. This time the heavy slug from the shotgun hammered into the center of the hulking beast's forehead. Bone cracked and splintered as the Sasquatch's head snapped back atop its neck. She leapt sideways as the beast's momentum carried it on forward. It flopped onto the ground next to her, twitching. Bethany wasn't taking any chances. She put another round into the backside of the Sasquatch's skull. Retreating a few feet, Bethany watched the beast for any sign that it might still be alive but it lay still in the tall grass, a puddle of red forming around its mangled head. Only then did Bethany look up and around to check on Benji and Stiles. Of Stiles, there was no sign. The dog handler was simply gone. Bethany knew exactly where she'd gone, to try to find her boys. Benji stood, frozen in place, tears gliding down his cheeks. His shotgun was held tight in his hands, his gaze locked on Quinton's corpse.

"I. . .I killed him," Benji whimpered.

Bethany slowly moved to Benji. The fingers of her right hand closed on his shotgun. "Release the weapon, Deputy."

Benji flinched as if she had struck him. His head jerked around to look at her. It took several heartbeats before his eyes truly focused on her and Benji realized who she was. He let go of the shotgun and she took the weapon from him.

"I. . .I . . ." Benji stammered.

"Now isn't the time," Bethany said. "Listen."

Benji shut up and did his best to.

In the distance, something cried out in the night. The noise was something like a shrieking scream. Nothing that could make a sound like that could be human.

"No," Benji whimpered. "Oh God, please no."

"Afraid so," Bethany warned. "That thing isn't alone out here. There are more like it out there somewhere."

Benji just stared at her, lips quivering.

Bethany slapped the hell out of him. He yelped from the pain of her blow.

"That wake you up?" Bethany raged. "Come on, Benji. I need you here with me. I can't do this on my own."

Swallowing hard, Benji appeared to come to his senses.

"Yes ma'am," he said weakly.

Bethany tried to hand his shotgun back to him. Benji shook his head at her and wouldn't take it. Instead, he walked over to where

Quinton's corpse was sprawled out in the grass. He knelt next to the body and very quietly said, “I am sorry, man. I really, really am.”

Then Benji got up and walked a bit farther into the trees to find and retrieve Quinton's AR-15. Benji readied the rifle, standing up as straight as he could.

“Let's go find those other bastards and make them pay,” Benji growled.

Bethany saw that he was still far from okay. She'd rather have this new rage-filled Benji though than the catatonic version that had existed only moments before.

“Follow my lead,” Bethany ordered and walked on, deeper into the woods.

Bethany shuddered as another inhuman shriek sounded from somewhere ahead of them. She was beginning to wonder if going after the other beasts was the right call. Now they knew what they were facing but remained in the dark as to just how many of the creatures there were. They could be walking straight to their own deaths. One of the things had been hard enough to kill on its own. If there was an entire pack or family out there, things weren't going to go their way. Still, it was their job to stop the damned creatures. They couldn't just leave them out here to keep killing anyone that was unlucky enough to run into them.

The rain was picking up which made it harder to keep an ear out for anything they might not readily see or notice other than by sound in the dark. It felt like the creatures had all the advantages. Bethany imagined that the beasts possessed far superior vision and hearing than humans did. They sure as Hell were stronger, faster, and tougher.

Bethany sighed. If they lived through tonight, they were going to have to come back out here again with the sheriff to clean things up and get Quinton's body.

****

Robbie's connection to the beast was unbreakable while he was asleep. He'd tried everything he could think of to wake himself from the nightmare that held him in its grasp. He breathed with the beast and experienced everything it did, everything. The killing of the dogs had been horrible and Robbie had been trying to escape the connection since it happened. After the beast had slain them, it hid itself among the trees. When it heard humans approaching it, Robbie could do nothing to help or warn them of the beast's presence. But it hadn't mattered. The beast he was connected to didn't go after the humans, who turned out to be a group of deputies and a woman to whom the dogs must have belonged. He could sense that the beast had wanted to but another beast, like it, showed up. This second beast was smaller, perhaps younger. It went after the humans instead. His beast held back and simply watched the attack. The deputies put up a damned good fight, losing only one of their number to the smaller beast before surprisingly managing to kill it.

Indifference was the best human word to describe how the beast Robbie was connected to felt about the death of the younger one. It watched the battle without intervening and even remained motionless in its aftermath when it could have easily moved in to wipe out the three humans easily, catching them off-guard and utterly by surprise. It certainly continued to be filled with boiling hatred for them. Something kept it from doing so though. It wasn't until Robbie heard the shrieks of still other beasts among the distant woods that he knew why. The shock that ran through Robbie's mind at their existence was like a splash of cold water striking his naked flesh. He mentally flinched and then had to recenter his thoughts. The beast made no move to join the others that were beginning to surround the surviving deputies. Through its eyes, Robbie realized that the deputies were people he knew. They were from his town. He'd even spoken to the woman leading them once when she visited his school. The confirmation that the beast was just outside the town he lived in filled Robbie with fear.

The dog handler came wandering into the clearing near where the beast had hidden itself away. The other beasts were focused upon the two deputies who had already passed it by without ever seeing that it was there. The handler lady must have found the remains of her dogs and was trying to get back to the deputies. Her skin was pale and tears welled up in her eyes. Her breath came in ragged gasps born from a mixture of loss and fear. Now that she was alone, lost in her emotions, the beast finally moved.

The handler lady never saw it coming as it crept up behind her with almost supernatural stealth. By chance, she turned to see the beast as its huge, hair-covered hands were reaching for her head. She screamed. . .but that was all she had time to do. The beast brought its hand together in a clapping motion, her head caught between their palms. Her skull was crushed like an over ripe melon. Chunks of bone and brain matter splattered everywhere as her head was flattened. The handler's body toppled over onto the grass. The beast looked at its red slicked hands and felt a deep pleasure to the point of almost licking at them. Robbie would have thrown up if he could have. There were no words for the mangled mess of bone and flesh that was left atop her neck.

As if in answer to his innermost prayers, Robbie finally woke up. His body shot up into a sitting position on the edge of his bed, howling like a tortured madman. If his parents had been home they surely would have come running thinking that he was dying. His body was drenched in sweat and bits of vomit clung to the front of his shirt. With a start, Robbie saw that he had vomited in his sleep. That scared the crap out of him. He could have choked to death doing it. It was only by the grace of God that he hadn't. The vomit stunk mostly of bile with a hint of the citrus flavor of the energy drinks he was chugging before surrendering to his exhaustion.

Robbie jerked his shirt off over his head and undid his pants, slipping them from his body. He left the soiled clothes at the foot of his bed and darted towards the bathroom, diving into the shower. He hurriedly turned it on and cold water flowed over him. Robbie shivered and tried to adjust the water's temperature. Shifting it too far, he mildly burnt himself before getting it right and then stood there, breathing fast, and getting clean. He knew now beyond any shadow of a doubt that it was time to do something. Keeping his nightmares a secret was no longer an option. As crazy as he might seem, Robbie needed to tell the sheriff about them. The question was how to do it in a way that anyone would believe him. Step one would be calming himself down. He considered going to Warren or Alison and getting their help, quickly discarding the idea of Warren. He'd just make things worse. Alison, on the other hand, Robbie hadn't figured out yet. She seemed to believe him but at others she treated him very much like a mentally ill person who needed help. No, Robbie decided, he was alone in this. It all rested on his shoulders.

****

Bethany couldn't believe they'd just killed a freaking Sasquatch, much less that there were more of the beasts in the woods with them. There was no denying it though. Inhuman shrieks sounded in the distance from just about every direction. Benji was with her but the guy was little more than a barely functioning basket case. His accidental shooting of Quinton had pushed him to the edge and likely over it. As much as she would have liked to leave his arse behind, Bethany knew that she'd never make it out of these woods alive without Benji.

They had to find Stiles before something happened to the woman. She'd abandoned them to go in search of her dogs. Bethany was heavily conflicted. Just moments ago her strong sense of duty told her that leaving the creatures out here without trying to stop them was wrong. If she did, the blood of anyone they tore apart would be on her hands. Bethany couldn't live with that. The more they trudged on through the woods though in search of Stiles, the more she came to realize that if they didn't turn tail and run soon, both she and Benji might not be doing any more living at all. The beast they'd killed was tough as hell and Bethany credited luck more than anything to them being able to take it down.

Bethany froze as she heard a sudden noise ahead of them. It was a strange and sickening sound. Bethany's gut told her that Stiles had just met an abrupt end. That meant another beast was just through the trees from where they were. Benji had come up next to her, stopping at her side. Bethany motioned for him to keep quiet. From the expression on his face, it was easy to see that he hadn't heard the noise that she had.

Benji was opening his mouth to say

something despite her gesture when the beast emerged from the shadows into view. The thing was huge, much larger than the one they'd killed. This one stood close to nine feet tall. It towered over them. The thing's body was all muscle and hair and rage. Giving a roar that seemed to shake the trees around them the Sasquatch launched itself at them. Benji shoved her to the side, charging forward to meet it. His AR-15 blazed on full auto. Bullets peppered the Sasquatch with dark spots of wet red. None of them got any penetration though. The wounds were all surface ones. Benji kept firing though as he closed on the monster. . . and a monster it was. Bethany knew the beast was a killer through and through. Benji was firing directly into the Sasquatch's stomach as he reached it, the tip of his AR-15's barrel almost touching its hair-covered skin. The Sasquatch didn't even bother to slap the rifle from Benji's hands. It simply leaned forward, scooping the deputy up in its arms. Hugging Benji to it, the beast crushed him to the point that blood flew out of his mouth like projectile vomit. When it released Benji's crumpled corpse, there was even a bulge of the deputy's intestine protruding from his mouth.

“Bastard!” Bethany yelled, leveling her shotgun at the beast. The weapon kicked in her grasp as it spat a heavy slug which struck the Sasquatch in the center of its chest. The slug flattened against the thick muscle there. Blood leaked out from around it. The Sasquatch reached out calmly to pluck the slug out of its flesh and fling it away. Snarling, it began to advance on Bethany. Working the pump of her shotgun, she retreated from the Sasquatch, backpedaling.

"Frag me," Bethany muttered, stunned that her shot hadn't done squat to the creature. That meant the pistol on her hip was utterly worthless. No way in Hell was a 9mm weapon going to stop the thing. As thus, the shotgun was still her only hope. Shifting her aim, Bethany took another shot at the snarling Sasquatch. Its head flicked sideways, dodging the heavy slug that came at it. Bethany gawked at the monster in disbelief. She attempted to ready another round but a hairy hand grabbed the barrel of her shotgun. Metal crumpled beneath the pressure of its grip, closing the barrel inward onto itself. The shotgun was jerked away from her.

Bethany turned to run but stumbled. She fell into the grass, hard, the impact knocking the breath from her lungs. Gasping for air, Bethany knew that allowing herself even a split second to truly recover would cost her more than she was willing to pay. As she rolled over to face the Sasquatch, her Glock slid free of its holster. She brought it up in a double-handed grip, aimed at the monster. While she knew that the pistol couldn't stop the thing, it might just buy her enough time to give her a chance to get the hell away. The Glock boomed in rapid succession as Bethany's finger worked its trigger as quickly as she was able. Her first few shots struck its torso without any real effect that mattered beyond seeming to make the Sasquatch angrier. Her shots worked their way up its body, the last ones striking at the Sasquatch's face before the Glock clicked empty. A bullet cracked the Sasquatch's left cheek bone. Another ripped a hole through its lower, snarling, black lip shattering the tooth beneath where it struck. Bethany's last round was apparently blessed. Though she was too flustered and fighting to regain her breath to truly aim, it punched into the Sasquatch's right eye. Wet pulp and blood burst forth as the bullet entered. The Sasquatch raised its head skyward, howling in pain and fury. When it looked back down at Bethany, its right eye was nothing more than a hollow, bleeding socket. . . and she was gone from where she had been. The Sasquatch looked to see her running like Hell away from it into the trees.

Low lying limbs snapped as the Sasquatch

barreled through the woods after Bethany. She didn't have to glance over her shoulder to know the hulking beast was gaining on her despite the small head start she'd gotten on it. Surprisingly, Bethany hadn't lost her Glock as she'd flipped over and took off like a sprinter crouching at a starting line. As she ran, Bethany yanked the only other magazine from her belt. Ejecting the spent one inside the pistol, Bethany slammed the fresh magazine home to replace it.

Bethany emerged from the trees into a clearing that appeared to come out of nowhere. Bethany sure as Hell hadn't realized she was running towards it. Bright lights lit up, causing her to jerk her left arm up over her eyes.

"Get down!" a deep, male voice barked at her.

Bethany threw herself flat on the wet ground. Rain pelted her back in heavy droplets. She heard the Sasquatch enter the clearing behind her. A deafening cacophony of gunfire erupted making her cry out, fingers of her left hand digging into the mud and grass, the other clutching her Glock so tightly that they hurt. The Sasquatch shrieked and wailed in pain as a barrage of bullets and shotgun slugs turned its body into a bloody mass of mangled flesh. The beast shook and jerked, stumbling backwards, before finally collapsing. Its heavy mass thudded onto the ground behind where Bethany lay.

A man ran over to her, kneeling down.

“You okay, Deputy?” the man asked.

Bethany looked up at him. “You're. . .you're Staker Blackburn.”

“Guilty as charged, ma'am,” Blackburn chuckled.

He was a lithe, though hardened man, not much older than she was. He had long, midnight black hair which was pulled back into a pony tail between his shoulders. A large, equally black cowboy hat sat atop his head. The boots he wore were heavy, military issue.

Offering her a hand, Blackburn helped Bethany to her feet.

“Now you sure you're okay?” Blackburn asked again.

“I'm fine,” Bethany lied.

Blackburn wasn't alone. There were over half a dozen other hunters in the clearing. They were where all the gunfire had come from, a coordinated blast that had taken down the Sasquatch chasing her. The hunters were whooping and hollering in triumph at slaying the beast. Their cheering drew Bethany's attention to them. She sucked in a startled breath seeing that the beast the hunters killed wasn't the one that had been after her. Both of this beast's eyes were intact and it was a good foot shorter.

Blackburn was sharp and alert enough to pick up on her reaction. “What is it?”

“That's not the one that was after me,” Bethany told him.

“It's not?” Blackburn said, not really sure what to make of her claim.

Bethany shook her head, not understanding how the beasts had switched places or what the hell happened to the huge one that had been chasing her. “There are more than one of those things out here.”

Blackburn smirked, “Oh we know. We found the one you killed before stumbling into you and that guy.”

Bethany stared at the lead hunter. “You know. . .”

He nodded. “Damn straight and we plan on getting the rest of the bastards before we call it a night too.”

“I don't think. . .” Bethany began to say but he cut her off.

“Don't you worry none, Deputy, we got this,” Blackburn assured her. “What's your name, anyway?”

“Bethany,” she answered. “But really, we need to get out of here, get the sheriff before. . .”

The beasts came out of the trees without warning. There were half a dozen of the things. Some of them smaller, standing only seven or so feet tall, and others a hulking eight feet or more. All of them set upon the hunters. A man in camo overalls died as a Sasquatch swung a clawed hand that ripped open his face. Another hunter was knocked over into the mud before a huge foot came smashing down onto his skull which popped in an explosion of gore.

The hunters were fighting back as best they could but it was far from enough. The beasts had the advantage of surprise and had used it to close ranks to the point of where even if the hunters brought their weapons to bear they stood a good chance of hitting each other.

A Sasquatch came directly at Blackburn in a maddened charge. The lead hunter was carrying a modified Barrett M82. He fired at the monster. His shot entered the center of the Sasquatch's forehead and exited the rear of its skull in a spray of bone fragments, chunks of brain matter, and splashing blood. The beast dropped instantly. Bethany felt Blackburn snatch her arm.

"Come on!" he yelled. "Run!"

****

Hawkins was still so excited to have come upon the Sasquatch corpse with Blackburn and the others. It was the high point of his life. All the years that Hawkins invested in trying to prove the beast was real were finally justified and brought to fruition. A small part of him resented Blackburn because he knew the famous crypto-zoologist and hunter was going to get all the credit for the find but tried to tell himself that it didn't matter. He had been there by Blackburn's side when the body was found and no one could ever take that from him.

Blackburn had led them on into the woods leaving the precious corpse behind though. After having a local deputy lead another Sasquatch directly into their line of fire, they were under attack. Killing the beast evoked mixed emotions in Hawkins. It was the scar of childhood trauma which made him a believer but even so, the beasts were living legends. Taking one of them down felt like killing one's favorite actor or rockstar. It had to be done, though. Just as Hawkins always tried to tell the overall crypto community, the creatures were far from peaceful. They were monsters that would tear you apart the instant you intruded into their domain. And now, they were under attack by a whole mass of Sasquatch. Jones had already gotten his face ripped up by one and lay dead in the grass. Tommy was dead too. A beast had smashed his head into a bloody pulp that slicked the bottom of its right foot and left Tommy's headless corpse spurting blood behind it. That same Sasquatch was coming for him next, stomping across the clearing towards him, getting closer with each passing second. Hawkins didn't have time to watch what was happening to the other surviving members of the group, Rick, Ben, Hawthorne, and Swaggert. He'd seen Blackburn flee the battle, dragging the lady deputy with him. The two of them were long gone out of sight.

Hawkins' AK-47 chattered on full auto. His bullets cut a swathe of shredded, bloody meat up along the Sasquatch's chest. He could see that the rounds were hurting the monster but they sure as hell weren't slowing it down. Hawkins jumped sideways at the last moment and the charging monster plunged on through the area he had been standing in. Hawkins swung his upper body around, opening fire again, peppering the Sasquatch's back with numerous bleeding bullet holes. His magazine clicked empty. Cursing under his breath, Hawkins discarded the rifle and went for his sidearms. Drawing the two Desert Eagles from the holsters on his hips, Hawkins met the Sasquatch's angry snarl with a feral, bloodthirsty grin of his own. The Desert Eagle in his right hand boomed, followed by the one in his left. The pistols were loaded with .50 caliber rounds. The first shot blew a chunk of mangled flesh from the Sasquatch's upper arm on its right side. That arm fell limp at its side. The second shot punched completely through the Sasquatch's left shoulder, jerking it back with the force of its impact. Hawkins didn't give the monster time to recover, pressing the upper hand he'd so abruptly gained. He walked calmly towards it like a gunfighter finishing a wounded opponent in the Old West. His third shot struck the Sasquatch in the forehead and ended its life instantly. The Sasquatch fell forward, slamming face first into the muddy ground. The rain that continued to fall was getting in his eyes so Hawkins shook his head trying to clear them. Blinking, Hawkins saw that the others weren't having the kind of luck that he was. That was putting it mildly. They were dead. . .all of them.

There were four Sasquatch left alive in the clearing with him. They encircled Hawkins, cutting off any chance of escape. Hawkins knew he was dead. He planned to take at least another one, hopefully two, of the bastards with him to hell though. The Sasquatch surged forward together, coming at him from all sides. Hawkins got off a shot that blew a gaping hole in the face of the Sasquatch coming at him from directly ahead of him. That was all he had time for though, before hair-covered, clawed hands were ripping at him. Hawkins wailed as his arms were torn from his body by two beasts on each side of him. The Sasquatch behind closed on him, yanking his head backwards to expose his throat to its claws. They sliced across the front of his neck, opening it wide, and silencing his screams of pain and terror. An explosion of blood sprayed from the gaping wound. The Sasquatch shoved Hawkins' body to the ground and then dropped to begin tearing into him with its yellow teeth. The beasts feasted upon Hawkins, ravaging his flesh.

****

Blackburn led the way, dragging her along by her arm, as Bethany was forced to keep up with him.

"The others. . ." Bethany yelped as they ran.

"Nothing we can do," Blackburn shook his

head.

She didn't know exactly how long they ran for. It could have been thirty seconds or it could have been an hour. Blackburn brought them to a sudden halt, though. The sounds of screams and gunfire was either too far away for them to hear anymore though it made more sense that those sounds had merely fallen silent.

“They're dead,” Blackburn told her, “And we're next if we don't come up with a plan and fragging quick. We'll never make it out of the woods if we just keep on running from those things. They'll overtake us and tear us apart.”

Bethany knew he was right but what the hell was he expecting from her? She didn't have a plan any more than he did and besides, wasn't he supposed to be the damn expert on the monsters?

“Making a stand here will get us killed just as quickly,” Bethany pointed out. “Those things are tough as hell.”

“You don't need to tell me that,” Blackburn snapped at her.

“We need something, anything, to distract the bastards,” Bethany said, looking around.

“Yeah,” Blackburn stared at her. “And just what the hell would that be?”

"Are you carrying any explosives?" she asked.

"You crazy?" Blackburn balked. "I'm a hunter not a fragging soldier in Iraq!"

Bethany was carrying a pair of flash bangs. She got them out and showed them to Blackburn. "Then I guess these will have to do."

"Seriously?" Blackburn didn't believe her.

"Yep," Bethany nodded.

"Help me," she urged him. "We need to get these in place."

Bethany handed Blackburn one of the flash bangs. "We're going to rig these to go off as those monsters come through here. They'll be after us so odds are they will."

"And where will we be?" Blackburn asked.

"Running for our lives just like we were," Bethany answered.

Once the flash bangs were set, they got on the move again. All their hope rested on the Sasquatch coming after them through the area they had just laid their trap in. If the beasts didn't, the two of them were just as screwed as they were earlier. If they did though, the flash bangs just might slow the things enough to give her and Blackburn a real shot at making it out of the woods alive. It was the best the two of them could manage with what was on hand.

Bethany and Blackburn took off heading south and east. Blackburn was impressed by the deputy's speed. He was having a difficult time keeping pace with her. The rain wasn't helping matters. The grass beneath their feet was slick. Blackburn had to be cautious to keep his feet from slipping and ending up on his butt.

They reached the edge of the woods, out of breath and slicked with sweat. Bethany stumbled out first, Blackburn on her heels. The Mullens house was only yards away from them. There were no lights on within its walls, at least not that they could see. On the road beyond the house sat the patrol cars and the truck that her people had arrived in. Blackburn and his crew must have entered the woods somewhere else.

Both patrol cars that Bethany and the other deputies had arrived in were there as well as Stiles' truck. Two of the handler's dogs sat near it on their haunches, panting, tongues hanging from their mouths. The sight of them hurt Bethany deeply in her heart. Stiles wouldn't be coming back for the dogs. She was dead. They were homeless now. Bethany promised herself that she would find them homes when all this crap was over. Approaching the dogs, Bethany wrangled them up into Stiles' truck and sealed them in its back while Blackburn watched. The famous hunter made no move to help her. Instead, he stood with his M82 ready just in case one or more of the Sasquatch were bold enough to follow them out of the woods onto the street. Thankfully, none of the creatures did.

With the dogs made as safe as possible for the time being, Bethany looked over at Blackburn. He met her eyes. Bethany nodded at her patrol car and Blackburn joined her there, sliding into the passenger seat as she got behind the wheel.

"What now?" Blackburn asked.

"We find the sheriff and get help," Bethany answered.

She glanced at the Mullens' house and prayed the family would be okay until they returned. Bethany cranked up the patrol car, shifting it into reverse. Backing up, she turned the car so it faced down the street towards the main road and then pressed hard on the gas. The patrol car took off like a rocket. When she felt it was far enough away from the Mullens' house so as not to disturb them, Bethany turned on the sirens and stepped on the gas even harder. Thankfully, there wasn't much traffic in a small town like

Clyde at this time of night. The streets were deserted. In just minutes, they pulled up at the Sheriff Department. Bethany had resisted the urge to radio ahead. She didn't want any of what they were about to share with Sheriff Amos leaking out because of some A hole listening to a scanner out there.

The patrol car's brakes screeched as she slammed them on. As soon as the car stopped, Bethany jerked its gear shift into park and leaped out.

"Hey!" Blackburn yelled after her, "Wait up!"

Bethany was already halfway towards the department's main entrance as he shut the passenger side door to start after her.

As she reached the entrance, there was a kid standing in the space between the exterior door and the interior one that led into the department proper. Not a kid, Bethany corrected herself, a teenager. She must have scared him half to death because he screamed like a banshee as the door was thrown open behind him.

"Who the hell are you?" Bethany demanded. "And what are you doing here?"

"I. . .I'm Robbie Lumley," he stammered. "I'm here to see the sheriff."

Bethany forced herself to take a breath. "Isn't

it a bit late. . ."

"I have to see him now!" Robbie yelled at her. "It's urgent."

Then he went white, blood draining from his cheeks.

"You're the deputy that was in the woods," Robbie said, staring hard at her.

"How the hell do you know that?" Bethany grabbed the front of his shirt, bunching it up in her tightly closed fist.

"The monster," Robbie was shaking, "I can see through its eyes when I'm asleep."

Bethany didn't know what to make of that statement. She'd seen enough insanity tonight to understand that not everything that seemed impossible this morning really was anymore. If monsters were real, why not kids with psychic powers too?

"Okay. . ." She struggled to remember his name though he'd just told it to her, "Robbie, come with me. We'll go find the sheriff together."

Blackburn had caught up with her but had kept out of her conversation with the kid. All three of them headed on into the department with Bethany in the lead.

Henrietta was at the main desk, which also served as the department's dispatch area. She was taken aback by the entrance of the bizarre trio.

“Beth!” she exclaimed. “What the hell?”

“Where's the sheriff, Henrietta?” Bethany nearly shouted. “I need to talk with him ASAP!”

“In his office,” Henrietta frowned. “What's going on? Where are Benji and Quinton?”

“They're dead,” Bethany started for the office door, “And a lot more folks will be too unless we get moving and fast.”

****

After his talk with Blackburn, Sheriff Amos had returned to the department. The level of insanity that was infecting his town had taken its toll on him. He'd gone into his office with the intent to finish up all the paperwork that the insanity brought along with it. Amos managed a good bit but didn't finish. Instead, he had laid his head down for what was meant to be just a second and fell asleep. His office door being flung open woke Amos up, hand grabbing for the butt of the revolver holstered on his hip. He didn't draw the weapon though, seeing that it was a freaked-out deputy entering the office.

“Sheriff!” Bethany shouted, storming across

the floor to slap her hands onto the top of his desk, leaning over to glare at him.

"Bethany," Amos said carefully, "I hope you have a good reason for barging in here like this."

"Benji and Quinton are dead. Stiles, the dog lady, too," she blurted out.

Amos blinked, part of him wondering if she was making a very bad and sick joke. Before he could respond, Bethany went on.

"There are monsters in the woods, Sheriff, real ones," spittle flew from Bethany's lips as she spoke. "They killed them."

"She's telling the truth," a young male voice cut in. Amos looked to see a teenager standing in the doorway of his office behind Bethany. "I've seen them too."

"Who's the kid?" Amos grunted, gesturing at him.

Bethany had to restrain herself to keep from slapping the hell out of the sheriff. "That's not important right now! Didn't you hear me? Quinton and Benji are dead and there are real freaking monsters out there."
"I heard you," Amos stared directly at Bethany. "Loud and clear, Deputy. Now calm yourself down or I'll escort you out of this station myself."

"But. . ." Bethany stammered, able to tell that Amos wasn't messing around. Throwing up her hands in a gesture of defeat, Bethany backed off, crossing her arms over her chest.

Amos turned his gaze to the kid. "Now, you want to tell me who you are?"

"Robbie Lumley, sir," the kid answered.

"And just what in blazes are you doing here, Robbie?" Amos asked.

"I know it sounds crazy, sir, but I've been having nightmares about the monsters in the woods, mainly just one of them really. I've been seeing through its eyes. Today, I figured out for sure that my nightmares aren't just bad dreams. I really am seeing through the Sasquatch's eyes in real time," Robbie explained. "I saw what happened to your deputies and how her and Mr. Blackburn made it out of the woods alive."

Amos looked from the kid to Bethany to get an idea of her reaction to what was being said. She had flinched and now wore a disbelieving frown on her face. Bethany might not believe but Amos could see that the kid troubled her.

"Don't you see, Sheriff?" Robbie spoke up again, "I had to tell you, make sure that you knew before the Sasquatch kills again."

Amos rose from his seat behind the desk. If

things seemed insane before, there was no question that they were now. “I see,” was the best response he could muster.

Blackburn made his way into the office too, gently ushering Robbie to the side so that he could enter.

“We killed several of them, Sheriff,” Blackburn said. “Bastards ain't easy to take down but they ain't unstoppable either.”

“And how many of your hunters died?” Amos scowled.

“Too many,” Blackburn lowered his head, shoulders slumping.

“We're wasting time, Sheriff!” Bethany was suddenly frantic again.

“She's right,” Robbie agreed. “I think. . .”

“Kid, did I ask you what you think?” Amos challenged Robbie.

“No, sir but. . .” Robbie swallowed, “I can feel. . .”

“You're assuming I believe anything you've said, kid,” Amos pointed out. “I never said I did.”

“He knew about what happened to us,” Bethany found herself defending Robbie. “There's no way in hell he could have known without being out there with us."

"And he wasn't, Sheriff," Blackburn jumped in, "I can attest to that."

"Fine, kid," Amos grumbled. "Say what you got to say."

****

Sheriff Amos had listened intently to Robbie's story about his nightmares and what the kid had seen. It was all just as whacko as everything else going on. He didn't really see any way to use the kid's connection to the beast, if it was indeed real, to their advantage at this point. It could come in handy later on though if things weren't wrapped up as quickly as Amos hoped.

Blackburn had been dispatched into the night to round up whatever other hunters that he could. Amos wasn't happy about that but they needed all the manpower and firepower they could get. The remainder of his deputies were called in and now they, along with the kid, were gathered in the department's meeting room. . . Harry, Hicks, Adams, Bethany, Henrietta, and Robbie. They weren't enough was all that Amos could think as he looked over them. He wondered if even the added men that Blackburn was supposed to be bringing back would be enough. Amos hadn't seen the Sasquatch himself but he believed Blackburn and Bethany about just how tough the monsters they were going up against were.

“And you really don't have any idea how many of these. . .Sasquatch,” Amos didn't like that word, it was just too messed up and surreal for him to be saying it in real life, “are out there?”

“I don't know, sir,” Bethany answered, finally having calmed enough to resume her normal professional demeanor. “I'd wager a lot.”

Robbie raised his hand like a kid in school.

“Frag me, kid,” Amos shook his head. “This isn't a classroom.”

“Oh right. Sorry,” Robbie was nervous and it showed. “I just. . .I mean I don't know but. . .”

“Just spit it out, kid,” Amos urged him.

“I think there's an entire tribe of the Sasquatch,” Robbie managed to get out. “In my nightmares, the beast that I am connected to seems to feel like it's an outsider, exiled from a really large group of them.”

“Can you be any more specific, kid?” Harry frowned. “Large group is pretty damn vague.”

“I think there might be forty or fifty, maybe

more," Robbie said. "I can't explain how I know that, it just seems right."

"Good God," Harry blurted out. "That many?"

Harry shot a look over at Bethany as if praying she would correct the kid and say that Robbie was utterly wrong. She didn't.

"Just how in the hell could that many of those things be living around here and no one ever know about them until now?" Harry raged.

"Who's to say we haven't heard about them and just never taken it seriously?" Hicks spoke up. "I mean there are stories about things out in the woods. I heard some of them growing up. My old man used to get creeped out sometimes when he'd take me hunting and he wasn't an easy guy to spook."

"That's fair," Sheriff Amos admitted. "I've been digging through old case files since all this crap started and I would have to agree. Those things have likely been here for a very long time."

Harry chuckled, "There's a reason you see all those master of hide and seek posters, I reckon."

Amos didn't find the joke overly amusing. Robbie must have figured out what he was thinking because the kid said, "Sheriff, I don't think you're going to have to worry about going into the woods and tracking the creatures down."

"And why the hell is that?" Hicks glared at the kid.

"Because, I don't think they're going to be staying in the woods anymore," Robbie explained. "Too much has happened. I think they feel threatened and that they need to make sure they're going to be left alone."

Bethany sucked in a harsh breath. "God help us."

At that moment, Blackburn came bursting into the meeting room. Everyone's eyes went to him.

"I got all the help I could, Sheriff, brought back another half dozen guys that we can trust," Blackburn sputtered, "But your phones are ringing off the hook out there. I got a bad feeling we're all in for more than our share of hell tonight."

"I'm on it," Henrietta jumped up from her seat and hurried out of the room to deal with the incoming calls.

"Kid, you gotta stop being right," Amos growled at Robbie in frustration.

"Guess the war's starting with us," Harry

smirked grimly.

"Everybody arm up," Sheriff Amos ordered. "I want y'all ready to roll out as soon as we know where we need to be headed to."

****

Jacob Mullens had watched the lady deputy and the weirdo guy come running out of the woods earlier through his living room window. They'd taken off in one hell of a hurry. His wife Sherri was asleep. The doctor had given her sedatives to put her out for the night. The loss of Susie hurt them both like hell. Unlike Sherri, Jacob was coming more and more to accept that she really was dead, her little body somewhere out there in the woods where it may never be found. The deputy's flight spooked him so Jacob had left Sherri sleeping and went to get his hunting rifle. After loading it, he stepped outside onto the back porch of their house. The rain had stopped but there was a chill in the air, left in its wake.

Taking a seat, rifle lying across his lap, Jacob stared into the trees of the woods behind his house. A wetness welled up in his eyes but he refused to allow it to turn into anything more. The way he was raised, men weren't supposed to cry. All he could think about was Susie. The sound of her laughter, how her face lit up when he came home from work, the feel of her little arms around his neck as he tucked her in at night. . . all those things were likely lost to him forever.

An inhuman howl rang out from somewhere in the woods. Jacob jumped to his feet, bracing his rifle against his shoulder. Through its scope, his eyes raked the trees in search of whatever made the horrible noise. What he saw made him shudder and almost pee himself. There in the woods, not more than a few yards away from his back porch, was a creature that stood around eight feet tall. It wore no clothes though its body was humanoid in shape other than its overly long arms. Those reminded Jacob more of an ape than a man. The thing had eyes that glowed yellow in the darkness of the shadows. Its sharp, jagged teeth gleamed in the dim light of the moon, black lips parted in a feral snarl. Jacob didn't hesitate. He squeezed the trigger of his rifle, taking a shot at the monster. It kicked, thudding into him. The bullet he fired found its target. The huge beast reeled backwards, blood flying from the wound opened up in its chest. Jacob worked the bolt of the rifle, readying another shot but lost sight of the beast. It had vanished back into the shadows. Jacob swept his rifle one way then the other, searching for the thing. It didn't make sense that something so big could just disappear so quickly and quietly.

Jacob wasn't prepared for what happened next. A completely different monster from the one he'd shot burst out of the woods to his right, charging toward the porch. Smashing straight through the banister that ran the length of the porch, the beast launched itself at him, clawed hands outstretched, reaching for his head. Jacob managed to spin around just fast enough to get off a single shot with his rifle. The high-powered round caught the beast in its sternum, shattering the bone, and plunging onward, into its body. The shot would have been instantly lethal to a human but not to the beast. The thing took the hit and kept right on coming. Jacob was left with no option but to try to get the hell out of its path. He flung himself over the porch's railing and went flailing into the backyard. Jacob landed hard, losing hold of his rifle, and having the wind knocked out of him. His rifle bounced out of his reach. Jacob scrambled to retrieve it but wasn't fast enough. The beast leaped from the porch. Only the door of the house being flung open saved Jacob's life. Sherri stood in the doorway, light spilling out around her, as she let out a shrieking scream at what she saw.

The beast forgot about Jacob and hurled itself back onto the porch at Sherri. She had no time to do anything before the beast was within reach of her. A clawed hand raked over her chest, tearing away her left breast. Hot, wet blood splattered onto the porch staining its wood red. Sherri's scream rose in pitch, now filled with pain, as the beast struck again. A second swipe of its claws savaged her throat, silencing Sherri forever. Blood spraying from where the front of her neck had been torn away, Sherri collapsed. Eyes wide, with her hands coming up in a vain attempt to stem the flow, her body landed directly in front of the beast. Roaring in vicious fury, the beast began to stomp Sherri's body into little more than a red pulp that smeared over the cracking wood of the porch.

"Sherri! No!" Jacob wailed, a fresh rush of adrenaline giving him back his strength. He dived for his rifle, snatching it up and fired at the beast. The hulking monster had seen what he was doing and jerked sideways to avoid being struck again. The bullet sent splinters flying as it hit the wall behind the monster and buried itself there. Blood was still pouring from the wound in the center of the monster's chest but if it was weakening, Jacob couldn't see it.

As he readied the rifle to shoot again, more of the beasts emerged from the woods behind him. Jacob heard the creatures before he saw them, whirling around just in time for the fastest to take a swing at him. Its massive, hair-covered fist entered him through the softness of his stomach, tearing through his guts, to burst out through his back, slicked red with his blood. Jacob spat red at the beast which didn't even bother to yank its hand that was plunged through his body free. Instead, the beast's other hand came forward, the flat of its palm against his forehead, shoving his head off his shoulders in a shower of erupting blood. Jacob's head went bouncing across the backyard.

The Mullens' backyard fell silent then except for the sickening, smacking, slurping sounds of the Sasquatch as they gnawed upon the corpses of the man and his wife they had just killed.

****

The calls to the department just kept coming in. Henrietta was doing her best to answer them all.

“Sheriff!” she called out. “The Sasquatch are all over town!”

The others, including Sheriff Amos, froze staring at the dispatcher.

“I've got reports of them at Waller's Grocery, the Heart cinema, the Exxon at the edge of town. . .” Henrietta rattled off, “And the things are all over the streets out where the Mullens live.”

"My God. . ." Hicks shook his head.

"We can't be everywhere," Bethany said.

"No. . .No, we can't," Sheriff Amos' expression was grim.

"My boys and I will go wherever you need us, Sheriff," Blackburn reminded him that they were there to help out however they could.

A couple of seconds ticked by before Sheriff Amos got his thoughts together and started barking orders.

"Blackburn, I want you and yours to get over to Waller's Grocery. Do what you can to help whoever is there." Sheriff Amos turned to Bethany, "I want you to take Hicks and the kid. Get on over to the school and see what you can do about getting it secured so that we can use it as a fallback position and trust me, we're going to need one."

"The kid? Really?" Bethany balked.

"Really," Sheriff Amos told her. "If he does have some sort of mystical or psychic connection to one of those things out there, maybe he'll sense them coming and give you some warning if they head towards the school."

"Hey," Robbie cut in, "I'm standing right here, ya know? And I'm not a freaking kid!"

"Stow it, kid!" Sheriff Amos snapped. "You'll be safer with her and Hicks than you will be if we just send you home."

"Okay," Robbie nodded reluctantly.

"Adams, you're with me," Sheriff Amos continued. "We're going to the movies. And everybody, listen up. I want all of you to direct anyone and everyone you come across to head for the school. Got it?"

His question was answered by a chorus of "Yes sirs."

"Uh, Sheriff," Henrietta called out as everyone started for the door. "What about me?"

"Lock every door into this place and stay here, Henrietta. Do what you can to give anyone who calls in some hope and tell them to get their butts over to the school ASAP," Sheriff Amos ordered. "If those things get in and you can't fight them off, get into one of the cells. They shouldn't be able to get at you behind those bars. We'll be back for you as soon as things are under control out on the streets."

****

Ed had managed to get a call out to the cops. Cowering behind the checkout counter, Ed's cell phone slipped from his sweaty hand, clattering onto the floor. He flinched at the sound it made.

On the other side of the counter, a hulking, hairy beast sniffed at the air and snarled. Before it were the sprawled out bodies of the man and wife who had been paying for their gas and picking up snacks for the road when the beast came bursting through the station's glass doors. There were shards of broken glass lying all over the red-smeared floor. They crunched beneath the beast's weight as it lumbered towards the cash register.

Ed knew he had to move. Staying where he was would be suicide. The beast was on its way to finding him if it didn't know that he was there already. Ed's eyes came to rest on the sawed off, double barrel shotgun below the register. He hated guns. His boss had showed him how to use the weapon though, in case one night someone tried to rob the place. Ed grabbed the shotgun and leaped to his feet. As he rose to his feet, he came face to snarling face with the monster on the other side of the counter.

The Sasquatch hadn't been expecting its prey to just spring up directly in front of it and that shock was what saved Ed's life and gave him time to swing the shotgun around towards it. He squeezed the trigger. The shotgun boomed, its thunderous blast echoing inside the station. At point blank range, the impact of its heavy slugs into the beast splattered Ed with its blood and sent the thing staggering backwards.

“Yeah, you A hole!” Ed whooped. “Take that, you bastard.”

Ed's excitement and feeling of triumph died as the monster sat up. There was gaping holes in its chest but the thing still sat up. It was moving slower but was still able to haul itself up from the floor.

“Oh crap,” Ed muttered. He aimed the double barrel shotgun at the thing and tried to fire it again. The hammers fell on empty chambers. Ed yelped and frantically tried to figure out how to reload the weapon. He saw more shells lying below the register. Ed struggled to break open the shotgun. As he figured it out, the monster was stumbling towards him. Seeing that he wasn't going to have time to extract the spent shells and get new ones in the shotgun, Ed threw the weapon at the monster. Swatting it from the air, the monster roared in anger.

“Oh God help me,” Ed wailed as he made a break for the station's shattered door, sliding over the counter. As his feet came down on its other side, the blood there caused him to lose his footing. He went down, face smacking against the counter as he fell. His nose crunched as his face bounced off it. Ed toppled onto the floor, pieces of broken bone flowing from his nose with the blood that was running out of it. The world was swimming before his eyes. . . growing dark. He felt more than saw the hair-covered hand that closed around his throat and lifted him up. Ed's legs dangled under him, two feet from the ground, as the hand that held him closed tighter and his throat collapsed from the pressure of the monster's grip.

Ed's body flopped back onto the floor as the Sasquatch released it. Looking around, it saw no more prey inside the station. Giving an inhuman howl, the great beast slumped to its knees, blood continuing to pour in red rivers from its chest wounds. The Sasquatch shook its head like a dog trying to dry itself and then heaved itself up once more to stumble out of the station into the night.

Meanwhile, across town, Blackburn and his crew pulled into the parking lot outside Waller's Grocery. Paul was driving one pickup with Blackburn riding next to him in its passenger seat while Brent rode in its bed. In the other pickup were Dale, Jack, and Ryan. The two pickups skidded to a halt as Blackburn stared at the scene straight out of hell that was unfolding in front of them. The entire parking lot was like something out of a warzone. The store itself was burning. Its bright flames lit the night.

Here and there survivors were desperately trying to stay alive but they were far outnumbered by the number of the dead who lay scattered all across the lot. A woman must have made it to her car just to have the driver's door ripped away and be pulled back out by clawed hands. Her gutted corpse was sprawled out next to the car, strands of her exposed intestines wetly glistening where they protruded from her open stomach. Not far away was the body of a man who looked to have tried to fight back. He lay face down on the asphalt, impaled upon his own hunting rifle, blood pooling around him. Another man's corpse had been discarded and left upon the hood of his car, its front window smashed inward by the top of his head. Shards of glass were buried deeply in the flesh of his cheeks and eyes.

"Holy. . .!" Paul squealed, knuckles going white from his grip on the pickup's steering wheel.

"It's a bloody massacre," Blackburn said quietly and then snapped into motion, swinging open his door and jumping out of the pickup. "Come on, man! We gotta stop this!"

A Sasquatch came bounding towards the rear of the truck. Brent saw the beast coming, training his AR-15 on it. He let loose on full auto spraying the snarling, hair-covered mountain of muscle. His bullets peppered the beast with small wounds but none of the rounds had the power to get through the dense muscles of its chest. All they did was make the beast angrier than it already was. The Sasquatch reached the truck and grabbed hold of it, flipping the vehicle over onto its side. Blackburn, who had just moved past the front of its hood, jerked around at the crashing sound of the impact and shattering glass. Paul was caught under the truck as it turned over. He cried out as the weight of the truck came down on him and Brent went flying.

Brent landed roughly several yards away, hitting the asphalt of the parking lot, hard, and rolling across. His right shoulder took the brunt of his landing, crumpling as the white of breaking bone pierced flesh. Gritting his teeth against the hellish pain, Brent managed to get to his feet, looking back to see Paul coughing up blood. Red poured from his mouth as he squirmed helplessly, trying to push the truck up off of him as if that were even possible.

Blackburn's M82 boomed, kicking against his shoulder, as he fired a shot that reduced the Sasquatch's head to an explosion of bone fragments, brain matter, and visceral gore. Even as the beast's corpse collapsed, Blackburn was moving, heading for the members of his crew who were getting out of the other truck. Dale, Jack, and Ryan were taking pop shots at the Sasquatch in the lot. So far the beasts were too intent on finishing up their earlier prey to care about their arrival. That would change quickly. Dale worked the bolt of his .30-.06 and put a round into the shoulder of a Sasquatch that was feeding on the body of what had once been a hot, young blonde. Jack was just standing, staring at the hell all around them. The blood had left his cheeks and he'd gone pale. Ryan was as crazy as ever. With a .44 Magnum in each hand, the bastard rushed to put himself between a Sasquatch and the mother and child it was chasing. He came between the beast and its chosen victims just as the mother threw open the door of the mini-van she hoped to get her daughter to safety in. If Ryan hadn't been there, the woman and child would have died right then. As it was, he bought them the time they needed to crank up the van and make a break for it. The van's tires squealed as the woman threw it into drive. Shooting forward, the van clipped a Toyota Camry in a space near it, crunching metal against metal, and then darted out of the parking lot, speeding along the road towards town. Ryan never got the chance to tell the woman that things likely weren't any better there. His attention was focused on the beast that was closing on him. Ryan's revolvers barked in rapid succession, one then the other. Each of their blasts ripped away chunks of hair-covered flesh from the Sasquatch's chest and shoulders. The beast roared in pain and anger as Ryan got even crazier. He ran to the Sasquatch getting in close enough to press the barrels of both his revolvers to the bottom side of its chin. Squeezing their triggers he sent the Sasquatch back to whatever hell had given birth to it.

Ryan didn't get to celebrate his victory. Another Sasquatch snatched him up from behind, thick arms coming together around his chest. It lifted him effortlessly from the asphalt in a bear hug. Ryan's ribs popped one by one, sharp snapping noises came from within his chest, each a greater surge of pain than the one before it. Screaming, Ryan struggled in the beast's arms, vainly trying to loose himself from its hold. The Sasquatch gave a final squeeze. Ryan felt his innards pushed up his throat as the middle of his body folded in, becoming nearly flat against the Sasquatch's chest. A thick cord of his intestines was pushed into his mouth, forcing it open. Ryan slung his head to the side as he died, the red slicked, purple bulge sticking out from between his lips rupturing to send brown shit splattering out of it.

"Frag, frag, frag," Dale was yelling. The sight of seeing Ryan die in such a horrid manner had shattered what was left of his mind. Dale had spent most of his life believing that Bigfoot was out there, chasing the mythical monster, but deep down he had never expected the creatures to be real no matter how much he wanted them to be. The AK-47 in his hands seemed useless and an utterly ineffectual weapon against the monsters he now faced, that were real flesh, blood, and bone in front of him.

"Snap out of it, you A hole!" Jack gave Dale a rough shove. "I need your freaking help, man!"

Brent was limping across the parking lot. His right arm hung at his side. It hurt like hell and he couldn't move it. Forced to leave his AR-15 where it lay, Brent had drawn the pistol holstered on his belt and carried it in his left hand. He doubted very much that it would save his life as a Sasquatch spotted him from the edge of the parking lot and came barreling at him. The beast loped in his direction, increasing its speed almost with each step. Brent saw that he wasn't going to be able to reach the others in time to get their help. Not that it mattered anyway, they weren't exactly holding their own. Most of them were dead already. Unless Blackburn worked some sort of miracle, all of them would be soon. Brent raised his pistol at the approaching beast, not even bothering to aim, and started shooting. The beast held no fear for the gun and the bullets hitting it did little more than sting. *Screw it*, Brent thought, as his pistol clicked empty. Who wants to live forever anyway, right? He was prepared to meet his maker when suddenly Blackburn was there, at his side, M82 pointed at the Sasquatch. The heavy rifle spat a round that blew apart the snarling monster's throat in a shower of torn meat and gore.

“Get to the other truck!” Blackburn shouted. “We've got to get the Hell out of here!”

“But the people. . .” Brent protested. “We gotta help them!”

“We'll be lucky if we can even save our own arses, man!” Blackburn said through gritted teeth, his M82 dropping another of the Sasquatch with a shot that tore through its groin. The Sasquatch clutched a hand over where its sex organs had been and howled a high-pitched, inhuman whine. Blackburn finished the beast as it dropped to its knees with a second shot that entered its forehead and punched through, out the back of its skull.

A woman who had managed to make it inside her car cried out as a Sasquatch rolled back its roof like an opening can of sardines. Blackburn watched as the beast reached in to get her and she hosed its eyes with a can of something that had to be pepper spray. The Sasquatch's head jerked away. The pepper spray didn't save her life though. Blindly lashing out, a powerful backhanded blow from the beast collided with her face. The woman's nose was driven flat with her cheeks before they too folded inward. Her corpse slumped in the driver's seat of the car as the Sasquatch forgot about the woman entirely. The beast clawed at its stinging eyes in such a fury that its own claws did far more damage than the spray had.

Blackburn popped off a shot that went completely through the Sasquatch's shoulder, splashing its blood onto the side of the car behind it. Jack and Dale opened fire on the beast too. Dale's AK-47 chattered, cutting a swathe of ruptured meat from the Sasquatch's groin to its throat while Jack's shotgun put a heavy slug into its side. Reeling, the beast half fell against the car, blood pouring from its numerous wounds, and finally toppled the rest of the way to the asphalt.

"Damn it!" Blackburn snapped. "We gotta go, people!"

The lead hunter sprinted for the truck Dale

had driven up in. Brent stumbled along after him. Dale and Jack rushed to join them but several Sasquatch moved into their path, others closing in at their rear. The two of them were suddenly surrounded and cut off with no means of escape other than fighting through the beasts. Dale's AK blazed away on full auto, Jack's shotgun barked, but neither was enough to stop the beasts. They were just too strong, too fast, and too many.

Blackburn and Brent heard them dying, screams of agony and terror as the beasts tore them apart, limb by limb. They picked up their pace. Blackburn got to the truck first but arrived on its passenger side. He tugged the door open and threw himself into its cab. Brent made it to the driver's side, pausing there, knowing that he couldn't drive well with just one functioning arm. There was nothing for it though. They didn't have time to switch things up.

"Don't just stand there, man. Get the hell on in!" Blackburn urged him.

The keys were in the ignition so Blackburn leaned over, cranking the car in an effort to make things easier for Brent. The big man grunted as he yanked himself up into the driver's seat. Putting his left hand on the wheel, Brent stomped on the gas. The pickup truck surged forward, Brent turning the wheel as best he could with just a single hand to angle its movement around towards the parking lot's exit.

There was a Sasquatch standing in the middle of the road leading out of the parking lot. Thumping its chest like an ape, the beast launched itself into a bounding run to meet the pickup head on. Brent's instinct was to hit the brakes but Blackburn shouted, “Floor it!”

Pushing even harder on the gas, Brent made no attempt to dodge the charging Sasquatch. Metal met the strength of primal flesh and bone. The truck's hood buckled and gave way as the Sasquatch's body broke. The jarring crash sent Brent through the window, to go skidding across the asphalt, killed instantly by his impact with it. Blackburn bounced back and forth inside the truck's cab between the dash and seat. When the motion stopped, Blackburn fell from the truck's open passenger side door. His left arm was snapped in two and bent at an unnatural angle. Several of his ribs were cracked. A long gash from one side of his forehead to the other leaked red into his eyes. The middle finger of his right hand was bent back completely and only attached to his hand by thin strands of sinew. Blood ran from broken teeth as he opened his mouth to scream at the sight of the group of Sasquatch approaching him. His cry was long and filled with rage. Blackburn heaved himself up into a sitting position. He had no weapon to fight the monsters with, unable to use even his fists. Blackburn looked around at the monsters, their black lips parted in snarls, yellow teeth ready to rend his flesh, and all he could do was laugh. His cracked ribs made it like sheer torture but Blackburn kept laughing. He was *the* cryptid hunter, *the* king of the woods and dark, creepy places. . . and here he was, helpless.

Several Sasquatch grabbed Blackburn at once. One beast ripped away his broken left arm. Another snapped away his right foot, ravenously gnawing upon it. Clawed fingers entered the softness of his stomach, sinking in to emerge slathered in a wet, redness after ripping him open from where they entered above his navel to just above his genitals. Blackburn had been looking down along the length of his own body, watching it all happen. At that point, darkness claimed Blackburn and he slipped into unconsciousness. The Sasquatch didn't care, he tasted the same either way.

****

Stella ran down the aisle. There was blood on her and she was screaming like a banshee, her lungs emptying themselves of all her breath. One of the monsters that had killed almost everyone in the theatre was after her, locked onto her scent like a homing missile. The thing ran straight through the rows of seats, sending those that it crashed into spinning away or breaking them to bits depending on how its body hit them.

Tonight was supposed to have been romantic. Her first date with Matt wasn't anything short of a full out bloodbath. His handsome features were taken from him along with most of the flesh of his face by the claws of a hulking, hair-covered. . .thing. Stella realized she didn't even know what the monsters were. They smelt like crap. . .animal musk mixed with urine, feces, and blood. No, they smelt like death, Stella corrected herself and that was what they dealt out with a vengeance to everyone in the theatre they came within reach of. A security guard, who was either really brave or an utter freaking idiot, stood his ground when the monsters entered minutes before firing a taser into one of them. The electric charge apparently wasn't enough for something so large to barely notice and the guard was rewarded by having the monster grab hold of his shoulders and literally bend the top half of his body so far backwards that his spine snapped.

The evening crowd hadn't been too large, maybe forty or so people counting herself, Matt, and the security guard. There was a lot of screaming at first but now the scared human voices were scattered and no longer a cacophony, hers among them.

Stella spotted a side door out of the theatre proper and zagged in its direction. There was another monster near the door but its attention was centered on a dad that was doing his damnedest to protect his daughter. He clutched the handle of a broken broom, hefting it like a spear, stabbing wildly at the monster that was trying to kill him. Stella knew if she tried to help the dad and his little girl, she would just die too. All Stella could do was run like Hell and pray to God that she made it outside and away from the monsters rampaging through the theatre. Her feet nearly slid from under her as she skidded around the corner of the doorway into the hall that led to the lobby beyond it. Clearing the monster near the door without any trouble gave her hope that she might just really survive the unfolding nightmare around her. Stella pushed her body even harder, pouring on all the speed she could muster as the creature chasing her came busting through the doorway after her. It was too large for the opening but the thing was a literal juggernaut and the sides of the doorway were splintered and broken by its mass shoving through.

The sound of a siren outside reached Stella's ear as she made it into the lobby. Stella yelped as she stumbled over the bodies of a pair of mangled teenagers and went sprawling onto the floor. She landed roughly on her elbows. Stella screamed again, squealing, as she heaved herself up, scrambling away from the dead. Her hands and the sleeves of her shirt were stained with their blood from where it had pooled around the two corpses.

The main, exterior doors to the theatre lobby hung askew from where the monsters had battered them down on their way in. Through them Stella saw the sheriff, carrying a heck of a big gun, and one of his deputies. They stood on the outside, cautiously peering in. They must have seen her too because the deputy started calling out for her to run to them. It wasn't as if Stella had any other option. Stella couldn't stay where she was or turn back without falling prey to the Sasquatch on her heels.

"Get down!" Sheriff Amos yelled and motioned for her to hit the ground. Stella threw herself flat on the lobby floor as a huge shotgun-looking thing in his hands roared, booming over and over like super close together claps of thunder. The blasts were so loud Stella thought her eardrums were going to burst inside her head. Clapping her hands over her ears, Stella stayed still where she lay, terrified to try to get up.

Stella felt the hands of someone, or something, grab hold, yanking her up. She opened her eyes, staring directly into the face of the deputy. His name badge read Adams. The first thought that crossed her mind was that Adams wasn't that much older than she was.

"You okay?" Adams asked, seeing the blood that covered her.

Stella nodded, head bobbing up and down frantically.

"Anybody else alive in there?" Sheriff Amos shouted at her as he stood reloading his weapon.

"I. . .I. . ." Stella wanted to tell them that everyone else was dead but she didn't know that for sure. What if the dad and his little girl somehow managed to escape the beast they were fighting? What if there were others she hadn't seen? Stella knew she'd heard a few other, distant voices inside the theatre proper. If she told them that though, they would either make her go back in there or just as bad, leave her alone out here.

"Damn it, girl! Are there or aren't there?" Sheriff Amos demanded.

"No!" Stella shrieked, tears running over the

curves of her cheeks. “Everybody's dead! Everybody!”

“Frag,” Sheriff Amos spat.

“I seriously think we need to get out of here, Sheriff,” Adams said, keeping his eyes on the doorway the Sasquatch that had been after her had come through.

“Get her into the patrol car!” Sheriff Amos ordered, “I'll be along shortly.”

“Yes sir,” Adams barked and took her by the arm. Stella didn't fight him as Adams led her outside.

Gunfire erupted in the lobby behind them. Stella refused to glance over her shoulder to see what was happening. She knew the sheriff had to be buying them time to reach the patrol car. It wasn't far from the main entrance. Its siren lights were on and flashing blue in the darkness. Adams opened the rear door for her and Stella slid into the backseat.

Sheriff Amos ran out of the theatre, firing a final shot at a monster coming at him from inside. He hopped into the passenger's seat, slamming its door.

“Get us the hell out of here!” Sheriff Amos barked at Adams.

The patrol car's lights switched to a white

color as it peeled out and then darted away from the theatre.

"Where to?" Adams asked. "Back to the station or. . .?"

"The school," Sheriff Amos answered. "If Bethany's got the place secured, it's as good a place as any for us to make a proper stand against these Sasquatch bastards."

Sasquatch, the word caused Stella to suck in a sharp breath. That was exactly what the monsters were. The big, hairy giants that had killed Matt fit the image that the word conjured up perfectly. As the patrol car raced through town, dodging turned over cars and abandoned vehicles, Stella sunk in the backseat. There were dead bodies in the front yards of houses, littering the streets and the edges of the road. She had seen enough death, up close and personal too, for the night and couldn't bear to see any more.

****

People were coming in from all over town, a fact that sure as hell didn't make Bethany's job any easy. Sheriff Amos had sent her, Hicks, and the kid, Robbie, to secure the school and turn it into, not just an emergency shelter for the town's populace, but somewhere that could somehow withstand an assault by the Sasquatch who were invading Clyde. The damn place was full of windows. Bethany had gritted her teeth in frustration realizing even with the inflow of refugees from the Sasquatch attack there just wasn't enough manpower to deal with the damn things, boarding them all up was impossible. The refugees were already gathering in the gym under Hicks' supervision. Admittedly, the gym had no windows and only a limited number of entrances to defend but Bethany still wasn't happy believing it was akin to putting all their eggs in one basket. There didn't appear to be another choice though.

She'd chained all the doors to the gym but the one Hicks was ushering those who were still showing up through and then left. Bethany stood outside the school's main entrance, staring out into the night. She was armed with an automatic shotgun picked up from the department's arsenal. The heavy weapon was equipped with a drum magazine containing fifteen rounds. Bethany found her thoughts drifting to Sheriff Amos. They hadn't heard from him yet. She wondered just how much trouble he and Adams might have run into at the theatre.

Bethany whirled around as a voice behind her spoke.

“Ma'am,” Robbie said.

“Jeez, kid! Are you trying to get shot?” Bethany shook her head, frowning at Robbie.

“I'm not a kid,” Robbie reminded her. “Stop calling me that.”

“Sure,” Bethany sighed. “What is it you want?”

“I wanted to let you know, the Sasquatch are coming,” Robbie told her.

“Yeah, I know,” Bethany looked at Robbie as if he were an idiot.

“No,” Robbie said firmly, “I mean they're coming right now. I can feel them out there in the woods. They'll be here in just minutes, maybe less.”

“I thought you said your mojo or whatever only worked when you were asleep,” Bethany challenged him.

“It's changing,” Robbie explained. “At least it seems to be. I can feel that. . .thing. . .I am connected to. I don't think it's like all the other Sasquatch. There's something different about it somehow.”

“Yay for it,” Bethany quipped snidely.

“Look, I'm serious,” Robbie pleaded. “You need to come on inside.”

Bethany knew the kid wasn't really so much concerned with her but rather wanted her present in the gym to help protect it when the Sasquatch did show. In the end, that was where she needed to head to and there didn't seem to be anything out here to do to help secure the school.

“Okay,” Bethany relented. “Lead the way.”

Robbie turned to head back into the school but froze in his tracks as an eerie howl rang out from the shadows of the trees just off the east of the school's entrance. A shudder ran through him and his skin went pale, blood draining away from his cheeks.

“It's here,” Robbie croaked.

“Well,” Bethany cocked her head sideways, popping her neck. “Maybe we should just head over there and kill the thing right now.”

“I'm pretty sure it's not alone,” Robbie said.

The beast from Robbie's dreams stepped out of the shadows into the schoolyard. It was the first time Robbie had seen the creature in real life. Bethany watched as the kid bit his lip to stop himself from screaming at the sight of it. . . and Robbie was right. It wasn't like any of the Sasquatch that Bethany had seen during the course of the hellish night they'd survived so far. It stood almost ten feet tall towering over the other Sasquatch which emerged from the woods to gather behind it. The hair covering its thickly-muscled body was different too. Streaks of grey ran through the thing's hair. There was a chilling air of both authority and intelligence about the thing. Its eyes didn't glow yellow or red like those of the other Sasquatch. Instead, they gave off an eerie green light that came from inside the beast rather than just being an effect of the moonlight reflecting off of them. Bethany shuddered looking at them. The thing exuded evil as if it were a living personification of it given flesh.

"What the hell is going on?" Bethany asked more to herself than the kid. "Is that one their king or something?"

Robbie was gawking at the grey-streaked Sasquatch too. "I. . .I don't know. Maybe the others are just afraid of it."

Everything in Bethany's training told her that she needed to get into the school, get to the gym, and make her stand there. It was her job, her duty, to protect the refugees gathered there. This night hadn't been like anything else Bethany ever experienced. Its events had pushed her to the limits of what her mind could take and beyond them. Bethany was ready for it to be over with. It had to end. Bethany's gut assured her that if she could take out the grey-streaked, big bastard, that it would be over.

“Go,” Bethany barked at Robbie. “Get to the gym!”

He saw that she wasn't joining to be going with him. Instead, Bethany was walking calmly down the steps from the school's entrance that led into the parking lot below.

“Ma'am!” Robbie called out after her.

Bethany ignored him, her focus keenly dialed into the grey-streaked beast and it alone. Robbie watched the deputy ready her automatic shotgun and saw that she meant business whether it cost her life or not.

“Don't do this!” Robbie moved down a few steps. “Please! We need you!”

The grey-streaked Sasquatch began to walk forward to meet her. The other beasts continued to hold back. Why was anyone's guess but Robbie thought it was because they were just as terrified of the thing he shared a supernatural connection with as he was.

Bethany and the giant Sasquatch stopped with only a few yards between them. They faced each other like gunfighters at noon in the Old West. Bethany's shotgun was aimed at the hulking monster. Its eyes flared brighter as the beast glared at her with increasing anger.

"Come on, you A hole," Bethany snarled. "Let's do this."

The grey-streaked monster growled, a low rumbling sound that rose up from its throat. It made no move to do anything but continued glaring at Bethany as if waiting to see how she would handle the lack of its response to her challenge.

The blaring of sirens made both Bethany and the beast turn their heads westward. The patrol car came out of seemingly nowhere. Whoever was driving it had the pedal to the metal. Its brakes screeched and tires squealed as the car slid to a jarring stop between Bethany and the giant Sasquatch. The passenger side door was flung open as Sheriff Amos got out, his own automatic shotgun thundering. The beast reacted with impossible speed, hurling itself away from the heavy slugs that blasted through the space it had stood in only a fraction of a second before.

"Damn!" Sheriff Amos shouted, knowing that not a single round he'd fired made contact with the huge Sasquatch. Then it was on him. A hair-covered hand reached low between his legs to rip away all of his manhood. Blood splashed on the asphalt of the lot below where Sheriff

Amos stood. He wailed, a high-pitched noise of pure agony, before the beast silenced him. As its left hand flung his genitals away, its right plunged into his chest, punching effortlessly through the ribs there. It came out clutching Sheriff Amos' still beating heart. His body fell forward into the beast. The grey-streaked Sasquatch brushed his toppling corpse aside.

The rear door was flung open on the other side of the car and a young girl that Bethany didn't recognize threw herself out, running like hell. The girl clearly didn't notice her or even Robbie standing on the school's steps. She wasn't making for either of them, her flight was directed only by the sheer horror that had to be flowing through her. Adams was out of the car on that side of it too. Aiming over the hood, he fired his AR-15 at the monster. Bullets ripped at the beast. Black lips snarling, it whirled in Adams' direction leaping over the car to land right next to him. Adams had no time to react. The grey-streaked Sasquatch tore at him with its clawed hands. Blood flew as they raked over his body, slicing deep grooves through his clothes and skin. Adams was shoved up against the side of the car by the beast's continuous attacks. His body bounced into it with each swipe of the clawed hands that shredded his flesh. Adams was a mangled mess of slashed up meat when the beast was done with him. Its grey-streaked hair was now covered in the red of his blood. Pausing long enough for its tongue to lick at red-smeared black lips, the Sasquatch returned its attention to Bethany as her automatic shotgun boomed in rapid succession like violent claps of thunder. Each of her shots slammed into the monster as she came striding towards it, her pace quickening with every step. Her face was set in a grim expression of hatred and determination, though tears were welled up in her eyes.

Robbie lost sight of the girl who had burst out of the patrol car. He knew her from one of his classes and thought her name might be Stella but it wasn't her that concerned him right now. The deputy, Bethany, seemed to have snapped. With the sheriff being killed by the grey-streaked monster, she was his best hope of surviving the night. Robbie couldn't let her throw away her life like she looked to be doing.

"Bethany!" Robbie screamed, sprinting down the steps below the school's main entrance, running to stop her. Either she didn't hear his voice over the booming of her shotgun or didn't give a damn because she wasn't stopping.

The grey-streaked Sasquatch was hammered by a barrage of heavy slugs that would have torn another of its kind to pieces yet it stood there, bleeding yes, but seemingly unfazed by the damage Bethany was inflicting upon its body.

"Die, you freaking bastard! Die!" Bethany yelled.

Robbie tripped running down the steps. His hands grabbed at the railing, missing it. His fingertips skimmed its metal but couldn't get a grip. He crashed onto his right knee, crying out. At that very second the grey-streaked Sasquatch grunted and took a stumbling step backwards from Bethany. Had she still been fully sane and functioning on a normal level, Bethany would have never caught what had just happened. Her snapped mind saw it all so very clearly though. The kid was more connected to the beast than he thought. At least she believed he was. Now she just had to test that theory.

Bethany flung her automatic shotgun away in disgust that it had proved useless and spun about, racing for Robbie where he was clutching his injured knee and trying to get up.

"Behind you!" Robbie shouted.

Glancing over her shoulder, Bethany saw the grey-streaked Sasquatch was on the move. Bethany's eyes went wide as one of its overly large hands reached to grab her.

Above where Robbie crouched, holding his knee, Hicks burst through the doors of the school's main entrance. With the skill of a professional soldier, the AK-47 in his hands rose up, braced against his shoulder. It let loose a stream of fully automatic rounds aimed for the grey-streaked Sasquatch's eyes. The monster roared and swerved away from Bethany covering its face with a thickly-muscled, hair-covered arm.

Hicks' interference allowed Bethany to put some distance between herself and the monster. Catching Robbie by the arm as she passed him, Bethany heaved him up the steps with her. He grimaced from the tenderness of his knee, left with no choice but to try to keep up with the deputy.

Strangely, instead of following them up the steps, the grey-streaked Sasquatch backed off. It retreated to where the other beasts were. They, uneasily, allowed the giant to join their ranks.

Hicks slammed shut the school's main doors as soon as he, Bethany, and Robbie were inside. Looking around, his eyes searched for something, anything to secure them with. The best he spotted was a metal handled mop on a janitor's cart that sat off to the side of the main hallway. Hicks quickly got the mop and wedged it through the handles of the two doors.

"That ain't gonna do jack," Bethany commented.

"You got a better idea?" Hicks snapped.

"I think I really messed up my knee," Robbie cut in. There was blood seeping through the cloth of his jeans.

"I know," Bethany said.

"What?" Robbie stared at her.

"Look," she urged both him and Hicks. "Look out there at the big guy. He's the one you're connected or whatever with right?"

"Yeah," Robbie nodded.

"That bastard is limping," Bethany's grin was wicked and feral.

"Oh no," Robbie raised his hands in a gesture of denial. "No. It can't be."

"Oh hell yeah, it can," Bethany chuckled. "Kid, you're the key to all of this. That thing just shrugged away nearly a full magazine of 12 gauge rounds but you hurt your knee and suddenly it gives up chasing me and limps back to its brothers and sisters out there."

"You're crazy," Hicks scoffed. "Both of you. Crap like what you're talking about isn't real."

"And Sasquatch are?" Bethany quipped. "Did you believe in them yesterday, Hicks?"

Hicks had no response to that and changed the subject, "That thing out there, why in the hell is it holding back? Like you pointed out, it could get in here easily if it wanted to."

"It knows," Robbie answered before Bethany could. "It knows that we've figured out just how deeply my connection with it runs."

Bethany whipped the Glock on her hip free of its holster, aiming it at Robbie's forehead.

"Whoa!" Hicks shouted, springing forward to grab her outstretched arm and shove the pistol towards the floor as she squeezed its trigger. The shot echoed loudly in the hallway as Robbie jumped away from where it hit the floor between his feet.

"What the hell!?!?" Robbie shrieked.

Bethany fought to get loose from Hicks and lost her pistol to him in the process.

"Don't you see?" Bethany spat. "If we kill the kid, we kill that thing out there too!"

"Damn it, Bethany," Hicks raged. "Even if I believe you, which I don't, killing Robbie would still be murder! You're an officer of the law. Start acting like one!"

Robbie wanted to run, to get the hell away from the deputies and everything that was going on. That was impossible though, so instead he moved to look through the window to the right of the main doors.

"Something's going on out there," he said.

"What?" Bethany growled.

"No idea but I am sure it's nothing good," Robbie frowned.

The grey-streaked Sasquatch was surrounded by the other beasts. They were shoving at it, as if urging the giant to do something, though God only knew what. The giant monster stood straight to its full height and gave a viscous snarl. The others gave up their attempts at whatever they were trying to do and retreated out of its reach, obviously afraid of the larger beast.

"We need to end this now," Bethany said firmly. "We can't stop all those things. Ain't no way in hell. They get in here and everybody, I mean everybody, is dead."

"We're not killing the kid," Hicks stepped to block Bethany's path to Robbie, still holding onto her pistol in one hand, his AK-47 in the other.

"She's right," Robbie said so quietly it was

almost a whisper. “This is my fight. That thing is here because of me. I don't know how or why but it is. I'm the one who needs to go out there and stop it before anyone else dies.”

“I can't let you do that,” Hicks protested.

“You can't stop me either,” Robbie said. “Give me a gun and let's get this over with.”

“Hell no,” Hicks shook his head.

“Hicks, you know this is the only shot we've got,” Bethany pleaded.

“Even if I give you a gun, Robbie, I don't think this Glock or AK are going to get the job done,” Hicks said.

“Give him your Desert Eagle, Hicks,” Bethany ordered.

Glaring at her, Hicks was still hesitating to give Robbie anything.

Outside, the giant Sasquatch roared and began to move towards the steps leading up to the school's entrance.

“We're out of time,” Bethany said.

“Fine,” Hicks relented, tossing the lead deputy her Glock and then drew his Desert Eagle, handing it to Robbie. “Be careful, kid. That thing's got one hell of a kick to it.”

Robbie took the weapon and removed the

broom that barred the handles of the door. The doors swung outward as he stepped through them. Bethany and Hicks watched him go.

"You know you've just killed that kid," Hicks scowled at Bethany.

"No, Hicks," she shook her head, "I've just saved us all."

****

The giant Sasquatch with grey-streaked hair snarled at Robbie as he came down the steps towards it. Robbie looked into its rage-filled eyes. Something had changed inside of him. He wasn't afraid anymore. The beast no longer held any power over him. Though he still couldn't explain the connection he shared with the beast, he now understood the thing's anger. Robbie remembered his nightmares more clearly than ever. He knew that the beast waiting at the end of the steps for him was once the leader of the tribe that lived in the mountains surrounding the town. Its mate had been killed long ago by the men of this area. As the years passed, the beast's anger grew more and more powerful, consuming its soul, until finally its fury had to be loosed. The tribe hadn't supported its actions. had exiled their former leader, casting it out. The tribe was only here now because the grey-streaked Sasquatch was so strong it would slaughter them too if they refused to join in its vengeance.

"Here I am," Robbie looked down from the steps at the monster.

The giant Sasquatch met his gaze. Their eyes locked and in that instant, knowledge was passed between them. Robbie's mind burned as he became aware that it was his ancestor who had taken the life of the giant Sasquatch's mate.

"No," Robbie whimpered. "No."

The Sasquatch growled, taking a step closer.

Robbie didn't want to die. He wasn't responsible for whatever his ancestor had done. He raised the gun at the Sasquatch. The beast knew his intentions through their connection and merely growled again, urging him on.

Whipping the pistol around, Robbie shoved it into his mouth, barrel scraping the roof of his mouth and squeezed the trigger. The top of his skull disintegrated. White chips of shattered bone, chunks of brain matter, and wet splashes of blood sprayed upwards into the night. Robbie's body slumped forward. The grey-streaked Sasquatch moved to catch it, taking him into its arms. Clutching Robbie's corpse to its chest, the beast howled at the stars above. Its body burst into flames. They burnt its hair away. The fat of its body popped and crackled in the blaze, flesh melting to ooze from its bones. Then the giant monster exploded in a shower of fire-blackened gore.

In front of the school and all across town, the other Sasquatch disappeared into the woods from which they'd come, taking their dead with them.

“It's over,” Bethany whispered.

Hicks looked at her, anger still filling his eyes, “Yeah, I guess it is and that kid. . . Robbie, he paid the price for the rest of us.”

“Come on,” Bethany said. “We've got people waiting on us in the gym. We need to let them know that they're safe now.”

Somewhere, far in the distant night, a sorrowful howl sounded in the darkness.

END

AUTHOR BIO

Eric S Brown is the author of numerous book series including the Bigfoot War series, the Psi-Mechs Inc. series, the Kaiju Apocalypse series (with Jason Cordova), the Crypto-Squad series (with Jason Brannon), the Homeworld series (With Tony Faville and Jason Cordova), the Jack Bunny Bam series, and the A Pack of Wolves series. Some of his stand alone books include Manhunt, Cryptid Park, War of the Worlds plus Blood Guts and Zombies, Casper Alamo (with Jason Brannon), Sasquatch Island, Day of the Sasquatch, Bigfoot, Crashed, World War of the Dead, Last Stand in a Dead Land, Sasquatch Lake, Kaiju Armageddon, Megalodon, Megalodon Apocalypse, Kraken, Alien Battalion, The Last Fleet, and From the Snow They Came to name only a few. His short fiction has been published hundreds of times in the small press in beyond including markets like the Onward Drake and Black Tide Rising anthologies from Baen Books, the Grantville Gazette, the SNAFU Military horror anthology series, and Walmart World magazine. He has done the novelizations for such films as Boggy Creek: The Legend is True (Studio 3 Entertainment) and The Bloody Rage of Bigfoot (Great Lake films). The first book of his Bigfoot War series was adapted into a feature film by Origin Releasing in 2014. Werewolf Massacre at Hell's Gate was the second of his books to be adapted into film in 2015. Major Japanese publisher, Takeshobo, bought the reprint rights to his Kaiju Apocalypse series (with Jason Cordova) and the mass market, Japanese language version was released in late 2017. Ring of Fire Press has released a collected edition of his Monster Society stories (set in the New York Times Best-selling world of Eric Flint's 1632). In addition to his fiction, Eric also writes a pop culture column for Altered Reality Magazine. Eric lives in North Carolina with his wife and two children where he continues to write tales of the hungry dead, blazing guns, and the things that lurk in the woods.

@severedpress
/severedpress

Check out other great

Cryptid Novels!

J.H. Moncrieff

RETURN TO DYATLOV PASS

In 1959, nine Russian students set off on a skiing expedition in the Ural Mountains. Their mutilated bodies were discovered weeks later. Their bizarre and unexplained deaths are one of the most enduring true mysteries of our time. Nearly sixty years later, podcast host Nat McPherson ventures into the same mountains with her team, determined to finally solve the mystery of the Dyatlov Pass incident. Her plans are thwarted on the first night, when two trackers from her group are brutally slaughtered. The team's guide, a superstitious man from a neighboring village, blames the killings on yetis, but no one believes him. As members of Nat's team die one by one, she must figure out if there's a murderer in their midst—or something even worse—before history repeats itself and her group becomes another casualty of the infamous Dead Mountain.

Gerry Griffiths

CRYPTID ZOO

As a child, rare and unusual animals, especially cryptid creatures, always fascinated Carter Wilde. Now that he's an eccentric billionaire and runs the largest conglomerate of high-tech companies all over the world, he can finally achieve his wildest dream of building the most incredible theme park ever conceived on the planet... CRYPTID ZOO. Even though there have been apparent problems with the project, Wilde still decides to send some of his marketing employees and their families on a forced vacation to assess the theme park in preparation for Opening Day. Nick Wells and his family are some of those chosen and are about to embark on what will become the most terror-filled weekend of their lives—praying they survive. STEP RIGHT UP AND GET YOUR FREE PASS... TO CRYPTID ZOO

Check out other great

Cryptid Novels!

P.K. Hawkins

THE CRYPTID FILES

Fresh out of the academy with top marks, Agent Bradley Tennyson is expecting to have the pick of cases and investigations throughout the country. So he's shocked when instead he is assigned as the new partner to "The Crag," an agent well past his prime. He thinks the assignment is a punishment. It's anything but.Agent George Crag has been doing this job for far longer than most, and he knows what skeletons his bosses have in the closet and where the bodies are buried. He has pretty much free reign to pick his cases, and he knows exactly which one he wants to use to break in his new young partner: the disappearance and murder of a couple of college kids in a remote mountain town.Tennyson doesn't realize it, but Crag is about to introduce him to a world he never believed existed: The Cryptid Files, a world of strange monsters roaming in the night. Because these murders have been going on for a long time, and evidence is mounting that the murderer may just in fact be the legendary Bigfoot.

Gerry Griffiths

DOWN FROM BEAST MOUNTAIN

A beast with a grudge has come down from the mountain to terrorize the townsfolk of Porterville. The once sleepy town is suddenly wide awake. Sheriff Abel McGuire and game warden Grant Tanner frantically investigate one brutal slaying after another as they follow the blood trail they hope will eventually lead to the monstrous killer. But they better hurry and stop the carnage before the census taker has to come out and change the population sign on the edge of town to ZERO.

www.ingramcontent.com/pod-product-compliance
Lightning Source LLC
Chambersburg PA
CBHW072238190626
46809CB00018B/2839

* 9 7 8 1 9 2 3 1 6 5 4 2 7 *